GEMMA JAMES

THE ZODIAC
QUEEN

SEASON ONE

THE ZODIAC QUEEN

SEASON ONE

The Zodiac Queen: Season One

Copyright © 2020 Gemma James

Cover design by Gemma James

All rights reserved.

No part of this publication may be reproduced, distributed, or transmitted in any form or by any means, including photocopying, recording, or other electronic or mechanical methods, without the prior written permission of the publisher, except in the case of brief quotations embodied in critical reviews and certain other noncommercial uses permitted by copyright law.

ISBN: 9798694647052

This book is a work of fiction. Names, characters, and incidents are either products of the author's imagination or are used fictitiously. Any resemblance to actual events or persons, living or dead, is entirely coincidental.

ARIES

BOOK ONE

PROLOGUE

Crushing grief. It's all I know. All I feel. The ache slithers through my soul, weighing down my bones and slicing me into a distorted version of the girl I used to know. Now there's just an apparition, a pale-faced creature whose flaxen braids belie a mature age of twelve. I hold my breath, afraid to breathe—as if the simple act of inhaling and exhaling will make this tragic reality *real*.

Each second crawls by in slow motion until my lungs burn for air. I suck in a soundless breath as movement surrounds me.

My uncle's feet hitting the floor in lazy, unhurried steps.

The burden of a stranger's gaze.

The dread that taints the air.

"You must be Novalee," says the stranger with the unfamiliar shiny black shoes.

I don't react to the statement, and Uncle Rowan's brows slash into fierce lines of disproval. "Please excuse my niece's reticent behavior. I'm afraid she hasn't been herself since the plane crash."

"It's quite understandable. Such a sudden tragedy."

They talk about me as if I'm not here. As if my shattered heart isn't bleeding all over the rug my mother loved when she was alive. I focus on the pattern underneath the pillow that cushions my knees, following the kaleidoscope of browns and royal blues as I smooth my sweaty palms down the front of the dress Rowan made me wear.

White for purity, I heard him mutter when he thought I wasn't listening.

He wanted me to look pretty for our guest, and even though I don't understand why I'm required to kneel in this stranger's presence, I don't mind because it means I can pretend he's not really here. I can be invisible like the heroines in my favorite fantasy books, cloaked by magic and imagination.

"Shall we get down to business?" asks the man standing next to my uncle. I give him a quick once-over. He's tall and broad, and I'm fascinated with the way his coppery hair catches the sunlight spilling through the arched windows in the sitting room. I've never seen such a color on a man before.

"Of course." My uncle gestures toward the archway leading into the study where my father spent most of his evenings. "Right this way, if you will."

They leave me on my knees, and I hear him ask the man with the copper hair if he would like a drink. For the next several minutes, the clinking of glasses and low voices filter into the sitting room through the ajar door, and I catch words that make my stomach sour with dread.

Words like *virginity* and *auction* and *marriage*. I fist my hands against my thighs, wishing I could roam the grounds with the birds and butterflies, but I don't dare move from my designated spot on my dead mother's prized rug.

Rowan is a strict enforcer, and I don't want to experience the stinging bite of his leather belt like Faye did yesterday for disobeying an order. Faye is my age and a daughter of a servant, but she's always been like a sister to me. We grew up together inside these walls, playing hide-and-seek in the countless rooms and halls. Before my parents' plane went down last week, we had free rein of the mansion and the surrounding grounds.

Until Uncle Rowan arrived and changed everything.

My parents have only been gone a week, both graves heavy and fragrant with fresh soil and sorrowful bouquets, but my uncle leaped into taking charge of our lands before the sun sank below the horizon on the day of the wake. I'm the daughter of a king, and now that my parents are gone, I'm the queen of a nation. A powerless child queen, because as my guardian, Rowan holds all the power.

"Why in God's name are you kneeling?" someone asks from behind me, his insolent male tone disturbing my misery. "You're not in the presence of the chancellor, princess."

I tilt my head and catch a hint of wild blond hair in my periphery. "My uncle told me to kneel."

"Do you always do what you're told?"

My brows pull together. "Don't you?"

"Much to my father's aggravation, no. But your obedience is admirable."

"Obedience was important to my parents."

"Then I suppose you'll be a perfect little wife someday."

The disdain in his voice piques my interest, and I pivot

on my knees to face him. His gaze meets mine, shooting a strange flutter of awareness through my chest. He appears to be in his teens, and just as I suspected, his dark blond hair surrounds his face in chaos, flopping over his forehead and threatening to hide his eyes.

And those sea-blue eyes are the reason for the sudden lack of air in my lungs. There's something about his stare that sends me into a trance. He circles me, footsteps slow and deliberate, and it reminds me of the way a lion preys on a prospective meal.

"Don't you want to get married someday?" I ask him, still wondering about his odd tone when he mentioned marriage.

His full lips slope into a frown. "What do you know about marriage? You're just a child." He gestures at my chest. "You don't even have a real set of tits yet."

Mortification heats my cheeks. "What an inappropriate thing to say!"

"The truth is rarely appropriate, princess."

"I'll kindly remind you I'm a queen, and you'll address me as such."

His snicker crawls down my spine with dark intent. "A queen on her knees. How...*appropriate*."

"Just go away," I snap, hating the petulance in my tone but helpless to mask it. He makes me want to grind my teeth, especially since I can't confront his rudeness with both feet planted firmly under me.

"Leave the sweet girl alone, Sebastian."

I startle at the presence of another boy. He halts in front of me, having come in from the gardens, same as the boy he called Sebastian. Through the open door, a breeze carries in the music of songbirds and the sweet aroma of plumeria, and once again, I wish to escape outside into the humid heat.

"I don't take orders from you," my tormentor fires back with that same irritated attitude I detected a few minutes ago.

"Someday, you will." The boy's coppery hair gives away his parentage, as does the authority in his tone. He seems older than his rude friend with the aqua gaze that makes my body warm and tingly in strange ways.

I avert my attention to the rug, assuming the older boy is the son of the man talking to my uncle in the other room.

Someone of great importance.

A leader.

Of course, I've heard whispers about the island up north where a group of powerful men reign in a circular tower twelve stories above the ground floor. I don't know the reason for their visit, but their presence scares me.

One by one, the sitting room fills with the opposite sex, ages ranging from early teens to adulthood. They surround me, eyes alight with curiosity.

"So this is her?" a dark-haired teenager asks.

"I expected her to be younger," someone else says.

Laughter flits through the room, the deep gruff too mature to belong to a boy. "And I expected her to be older." I catch the emerald gaze of the boy...*man*...who laughed at my age. He must be a decade older than me.

And now I'm fidgeting, twirling two tiny blond braids around my finger as I try not to squirm under their stares.

"By the time the queen turns eighteen," the boy with the copper hair says, "the age difference won't matter." He closes the distance between us and covers my hand, putting a stop to my nervous braid-twirling. Returning my hands to my lap, I nibble my bottom lip as he pets the top of my head.

"What happens when I turn eighteen?"

He takes me by the chin, fingers warm and gentle. "Upon your eighteenth birthday, my queen, you'll belong to us."

1

PRESENT-DAY, MARCH 21ST

The road is smooth under the wheels of the limousine, unhindered by bumps or potholes. Not that I'd know much about either. I've been surrounded by the absolute best from the moment I came out of the womb. Artisan furniture made of quality wood and fine leather. Enough jewelry to match every hue of nail polish in existence. Collections of the latest couture—a wardrobe large enough to need its own wing.

It took several chests to contain even a tenth of my clothing. Uncle Rowan said he'd send the rest at a later date. In the meantime, he promised a shopping spree with my ladies after we settle on Zodiac Island. Maybe if I weren't visiting the small nation in metaphorical chains, the prospect of new clothing and jewels would excite me.

"It's so beautiful," Elise says, awe dripping from her tone as we pull between the iron gates of the estate that houses all twelve members of the Brotherhood. Eyes widening with excitement, she pushes her wispy blond bangs to the side to get a better look.

The castle-like structure sits atop a hillside. Arched mullion windows line the floors in neat, perfect rows, charming those who gaze upon the estate. It really is a gorgeous place, down to the ivory stonework. I can't help but turn away from the sight with a sickness in the pit of my gut.

"It looks like a prison," Faye gripes, her fuchsia-hued lips forming a scowl. Her words echo my thoughts.

Elise glances my way, rose coloring her cheeks, baby blues deepening with an apology. "I'm sorry. That was an insensitive thing to say."

"Don't apologize for appreciating beautiful architecture." I cross my right ankle over my left. "All we can do is make the best of the situation."

"It's so unfair," Faye complains in a harsh whisper. "You shouldn't have to go through this."

None of us should.

Though she didn't say the words, they flit through my mind anyway. It's what she meant, but as one of my ladies, she's been trained to put me first, to push aside her personal thoughts, feelings, and opinions in favor of my wants and needs.

Elise is ecstatic at the prospect of landing a husband on Zodiac Island. But Faye is here against her wishes, as am I. She was forced to leave the love of her life with the expectation that she marry above her station—an opportunity not gifted to many servants.

As we roll down the long driveway, trees rustle in the breeze on either side in blankets of grass. The lawns are lush and green from the abundant rain for which Zodiac Island is famous. Just behind the towering estate and past the cliffs, I spy the ocean. That endless stretch of water is the only thing that brightens this reality for me.

I've never lived so close to the sea. On the drive over from the Brotherhood's private airstrip, I spotted the most beautiful beaches, the waters a deep cobalt with miles of uncluttered sand inviting one to search for sand dollars and seashells.

Uncle Rowan promised I'd have some freedom on this God-forsaken chunk of rock—the chance to roam and explore. In theory, it's an alluring idea, but I can't stop the niggle of dread chasing me. The closer I come to meeting the chancellor, whom I'll spend the next month with, the more my belly roils with nervous energy. No amount of adventurous discovery on new soil will make this forced marriage worth it. Not considering the rumors about the Brotherhood that have run rampant on a global level.

Political corruption.

Sex scandals.

And the thing that worries me most—the gross negligence of women's rights.

As we come to a stop at the main entrance, I can't deny the fear gripping me. Palms clammy, I try to draw in a deep breath but fail.

Faye grasps my fingers and squeezes. "Just breathe. We're right here with you."

I've known about this inevitable day for six years. Six long years of my uncle drilling it into my brain at every turn, trying to prepare me so it would be easier to accept.

It's not, and I'm far from prepared.

We roll to a stop and the engine shuts off. The resulting quiet is as unsettling as my thoughts. Doors open and close, and seconds later, Rowan swings mine open. I glare at him through the hot tears flooding my eyes. Oh, how I despise those drops of weakness as they slip past my armor.

His stature is immovable, as is his will. "Dry your eyes, child."

"I'm not a child."

"You're right. You're a grown lady, and it's time you stop the theatrics and behave like the queen I trained you to be."

"Don't make me do this." I bite my lip to keep from adding a whiny "please" at the end of that sentence. Despite what my uncle might think of me, I'm not this pathetic.

Not usually.

What I am is desperate...which is pathetic in its own right.

"It was done six years ago, Novalee."

"Undo it."

"That isn't an option."

The urge to run is strong. Craning my neck, I study my surroundings from the back seat of the vehicle. The grounds seem endless from this vantage point, but even if I hide amongst the trees long enough to evade, where will I go? I'm on foreign soil, the terrain unfamiliar, and finding a stranger willing—or stupid enough—to go against the Brotherhood by helping me will be next to impossible.

And it's not like I haven't tried running before.

"Don't try it, child," Rowan warns in a dark tone. "Running will only delay the inevitable and leave you unable to sit." Gripping me by the arm, he drags me from the luxurious vehicle before letting the door slam shut with the kind of finality that inspires teeth-grinding.

I'm angry and indignant and desperate to stop the tears

from escaping down my cheeks. What an utter fool I was in thinking I could get through this without falling apart. I've straddled the line of a nervous breakdown since I turned eighteen two months ago when my uncle and his men thwarted my last escape attempt. No amount of begging had saved me from a brutal session with Rowan's whip, and it won't save me from what he claims is my *duty*.

And he's gone above and beyond over the years to make sure this day happens, going so far as to drive away anyone who might be an ally. Kitchen staff, servants, even Angeles, the old man who used to tend the gardens and was like a grandfather to me.

All of them, gone.

Save for my ladies, I'm alone in this. Faye and Elise exit the limo and flank me on either side, and the three of us stand as a united front. Their presence is a comfort, but I still can't help but wish the ground would open and let the soil bury me.

Panic is just a few breaths away.

I've never been touched by a boy, and the thought of being at the mercy of twelve experienced men is horrifying. My only saving grace is the terms of the contract, which prohibits them from taking my virtue until the night of the wedding.

With a displeased frown, Rowan hands me a handkerchief. "You are minutes away from meeting Chancellor Castle. Don't embarrass yourself."

I yank his offering from his hand and dab at my wet eyes. "This is wrong. My parents wouldn't have wanted this for me."

"Your parents aren't here."

"Why are you doing this? Is it the money?"

"My dear, innocent Novalee. The money is a bonus, but while you're locked away here, serving the Brotherhood, you'll be out of sight and out of mind. Someone has to rule our lands."

After all the times I've pleaded for an answer, I'm shocked to get one now, and it's confirmation of what I suspected to be true. Uncle Rowan wants my title, and with me gone, he has a better chance of securing the permanent transfer of power. Twelve months is a long time to be absent, especially amid such political uncertainty.

"Come," he says, taking me by the arm as a young woman appears from the iron doors of the estate, dressed in full maid uniform. "The chancellor awaits." He urges me forward, and the metaphorical chains that bind me tighten to an intolerable level.

This is happening.

My ladies can't protect me from it.

My uncle refuses to stop it.

And the only two people who would have done anything to ensure my happiness—even if it meant moving the stars and planets—died six years ago.

As the maid ushers us into my prison for the next twelve months and beyond, I have no choice but to let destiny drag me into the den.

2

For a prison, the Zodiac Estate is nothing short of awe-inspiring. The grand foyer is open, light, and airy, and smack in the middle stands a white stone staircase. To my right, a waterfall cascades down a rocky wall.

"Wow," Elise breathes, and I can't help but share in her awe.

I tilt my head and squint from the bright rays pouring through the circular skylight which spans the foyer and second-floor atrium. The stained glass is sectioned into twelve slices—one representing each sign of the zodiac, from the ram to the fishes. It's beautiful and immaculate and...

"It's cold," Faye says, plucking the word from my mind.

Gooseflesh erupts on my skin, and I'm not sure if it's from the chilly breeze spilling into the foyer with our arrival, or the thought of what waits for me behind closed doors. Just past the wall of bubbling water, I spot an archway leading into what looks like an industrial-sized kitchen. The maid ushers us in the opposite direction, through a door on the left and down a long hallway, and we enter a library. My eyes widen at the sheer massiveness of the bookshelves—rows upon rows of spines showing a varied and eclectic collection.

A man rises from behind a desk, the wood heavy and dark with an edge of masculinity, and Uncle Rowan steps forward. "Chancellor, I'm honored to present my niece, Novalee Van Buren."

The chancellor nods at me in greeting. "Welcome to Zodiac Island. You may call me Liam."

Dipping my head in acknowledgment, I study him from beneath my lashes. His coppery hair niggles at a memory, digging at the layers of time until I recall the younger version of the man standing before me.

At age twelve, I didn't quite grasp the devastating sexiness of Liam Castle, but now it hits me full-on, and I feel his hot-blooded gaze in every nerve ending.

"Do you remember me, Novalee?"

"I remember you."

"You've grown into a beautiful woman." His attention heats my skin under the white skirt and sweater Uncle Rowan insisted I wear.

"Thank you."

He gestures toward his maid. "Selma, escort the queen's ladies to their quarters to freshen up. Dinner begins at six."

I cast an anxious glance at Faye and Elise. I want them at my side, a buffer between this imposing man and me. "I'd rather they stay."

"You'll be reunited soon enough." His tone is decisive. Final. An authoritative nod of his beautiful head sends the maid into motion, and she escorts my ladies through the library door. An unsettling disquiet descends until Liam gestures toward a group of suede leather chairs. "Shall we sit?"

That's when I spot a manila envelope sitting on a table. Undoubtedly, it's the contract my uncle signed a week after my parents' plane went down, promising my hand in marriage to the Zodiac Brotherhood.

Rowan places a palm at the small of my back, urging me forward. After we settle into the chairs—my uncle and I facing the chancellor—Liam removes several pieces of paper from the envelope and lays one on the table between us. The scrawl of Rowan's signature ignites a deep ache in my gut. That ink is a reminder of all I lost.

I swallow hard. Not even six years can erase the reality of my parents' deaths or the gaping hole their absence created in my life.

Liam removes a pen from the pocket of his expensive charcoal suit and hands it to Rowan. "As you discussed with my father six years ago, by signing, you declare Novalee has remained a virgin."

I hold my breath as my uncle's hand hovers over the line at the bottom. One flick of his wrist and a little ink, and life as I know it will change forever. That ink will be the start of the end.

Fighting tears, I watch my uncle scrawl his name across the bottom. He sets the pen down carefully, paying small homage to the significance of this moment and the destruction ricocheting through my heart.

"Excellent," Liam says as he stands. "Before you take your leave, I need a show of good faith from Novalee."

I'm trying not to wither under the chancellor's scrutinous stare when my uncle asks the only question in my head.

"What do you have in mind?"

Liam's light brown eyes refuse to waver from mine. "A sexual favor as a show of her commitment to the contract. Her virginity will remain intact, of course."

I jump to my feet. "I will do no such thing!" It's a gut-instinct reaction—an absurd one if I take into account what will be expected of me in the next twelve months.

"You'll do it because I demand it." Liam's brow arches in challenge.

My uncle stands, shooting me a look of warning. "Remember your place, dear niece."

"My place?" I cross my arms, incredulous, and glare at both of them. "And what exactly is my *place*?"

"That would be on your knees," Liam says, taking a step closer.

"Why? Because you're the *chancellor*?" I challenge in a scathing tone, knowing full well my mouth will get me into serious trouble with this man if I'm not careful.

"No, my queen. My reasons are a matter of logistics."

"Logistics?" I say unbelievingly.

"Yes. The position will provide more efficient use of your mouth."

I turn to my uncle. "You can't allow this!" The plea echoes, and I'm positive everyone on the first floor hears my outburst.

Rowan sets a heavy hand on my shoulder. "Obedience to the Brotherhood is your duty, Novalee. Kneel before the chancellor."

I stiffen my legs, refusing to submit even as my eyeballs

burn from the impossibility of the circumstances. I want to plead again, but no amount of begging for a different outcome will make the resolution on either man's face waver.

Because there is no freedom on this island.

No rights as queen of a foreign nation.

No *choice*.

The unyielding weight of my uncle's grip sends me to my knees. My chest heaves with indignation as Liam towers in front of me, hands at his back, shoulders wide as the bulge behind his zipper taunts me with what I'll face for the next twelve months.

Twelve men.

Headstrong and virile.

And all of them determined to own me.

Rowan clears his throat. "I apologize for my niece's lack of protocol."

I resist gnashing my teeth.

"She'll learn." Liam pets my head as if I'm a prized Pomeranian. "It'll take some time, but she'll adapt to our customs."

"Yes, well, I'm afraid Novalee is a very strong-willed young woman."

"I assure you, that is an issue I intend to address."

I cast one last pleading look at my uncle, but the stern line of his mouth fails to give me hope.

"I'll wait in the parlor while the two of you become acquainted," he says, and I'm helpless as I watch my final shred of hope disappear through the door. It slams upon his exit, and I jump. The ensuing silence is too invasive. Too consuming.

Liam doesn't move or speak at first. Neither do I. The seconds tick past as I study his dark gray trousers, purposefully keeping my focus below his zipper. His heightened breathing fractures the quiet, the inhales and exhales shallow and gruff, laden with a hint of what I think is desire.

Has anyone ever sounded so...aroused in my presence before? Stood in front of me like this—with masculine power and appeal? Six years ago, Liam did, though now I realize he held himself back in deference to my age.

"Eyes up here." His commanding tone rumbles through my bones, drawing my gaze to his face, and there's no denying how gorgeous he is. Strong jaw, neatly trimmed beard, and that coppery hair I remember from six years ago when he scolded the boy with the wild blond hair. This man stood up for me back then, but that won't be the case this time.

"You've come a long way since that child on her knees," he says as if our minds are on the same wavelength. He smoothes a palm down the back of my head. "It's okay to be unsure. I know you're untouched and innocent. I'm honored to be the first to touch you."

Except he'll do more than touch me. Once again, my attention falls to his pants and the noticeable outline of his erection.

Erection.

I'm not unfamiliar with the word. I know how the male anatomy works. I even know what's expected of me. As if to confirm my suspicion, he unbuckles his belt and unfastens his pants.

"Unbutton your top, Novalee."

My fingers visibly shake as I reach for the first button,

and it takes three tries before it slips free of the loop. I undo the next two then look at him for instruction, hoping he'll allow me to stop at showing cleavage.

"Keep going."

Gulping past the tightness in my throat, I reveal more skin. The material parts, exposing my satin brassiere. Liam tugs on the blouse, one brow arched in silent command, and I let the top slip off my shoulders.

"Take off the undergarment too."

The urge to beg is intense, a plea for my modesty on the tip of my tongue, and I hesitate a second too long.

"I don't issue orders twice," he says, gripping me by the chin. "I'll make this as easy on you as I can, but this is your only warning."

His tone is harsh, stabbing like a knife to my gut, and before he can give the command again—and punish me for it—I remove the last piece of material covering my breasts. A draft of air caresses my nakedness, coaxing my nipples to bud. I've never felt more vulnerable than I do now, on my knees and naked from the waist up.

Liam draws in an appreciative breath. "Stunning." He grabs my wrists and forces my hands to my chest. "Play with your nipples."

"Why?" I whisper.

"Don't question me."

I'm utterly humiliated as I fondle my nipples, gently rolling the sensitive peaks between thumb and forefinger.

"Good girl," he breathes, reaching for the stretchy material of his boxer briefs. He exposes himself, and at the first sight of his shaft, my eyes bulge.

"It's big."

"You'll learn to take it."

I don't see how. He's thick and long, and his fist doesn't cover half the length as he folds his fingers around it. I can't hide a nervous gulp.

"Will you be gentle?"

With his free hand, he palms my face, the brush of his thumb a caress on my cheekbone. "Compared to some of my brothers, I'll be merciful."

And that's where the gentleness of his touch stops.

Fisting my hair, he yanks my head back, and the position angles my face just right, his harsh grip ensuring I can't escape his hold.

"Please," I gasp, despising myself for the slip-up. "I don't know how to do this."

"Your inexperience is what draws me." He strokes his length, confident in his skill as he moves his hand from root to tip and back again. "Pinch your nipples."

I follow his command, adding more pressure to the flesh between my fingers. A curious warmth darts between my thighs. I once touched myself, bringing about the same tingly rush spreading through my bones now, but my sense of embarrassment was too strong, and I stopped before it went any further.

"Harder. Make them ache."

Maybe if I make my nipples hurt, the warmth between my legs will go away. I press down hard, face tightening from the hot pain radiating through my breasts.

The wet tip of his erection pushes against my lips. "Taste me," he says, pulling my hair until I dart out my tongue.

He's salty with a hint of bittersweet, and I'm not sure if

I like the taste or not. I lick my lips clean, and then his flesh is there again, pressing against my lips until they part and allow him entrance. My mouth closes around the plump head, and he sucks in a sharp breath between his teeth.

"Jesus," he mutters. "So sweet."

And then he starts to thrust, his raspy voice shooting out curt instructions like *suck* and *no teeth* and *gag for me*. That last command confuses me until he pushes toward the back of my throat, and I realize he means to go deep.

Too deep.

Instinct kicks in, and I push my tongue against the hot flesh in my mouth.

"Don't fight me," he says with a low growl, pulling out and slapping his dick against my cheek. "My brothers won't be as gentle and patient as me. They'll tire of your teasing and take their pleasure from your ass." He thrusts into my throat again, only this time when the gagging starts, I fight to accept it.

To accept *him*.

"This is for your own good, my sweet girl."

He sets the tempo with quick jabs, and my chest aches from gagging on his girth. Humiliation clogs my nose, making breathing difficult with the way he's claiming my mouth. I peek up, desperation a scream on my face, and our eyes meet. His are darker than a moonless night, lids at half-mast.

He seems...entranced. Caught up in a spell. A curious sense of power takes hold of me. I've never felt anything like it before.

And I've never witnessed anything as beautiful as the surrender in a man like Liam.

His hand tightens in my hair, and with a final jerk between my tonsils, he goes still. "Swallow," he groans as his hot release spurts into my throat. I choke a little as it slides down. Afterward, he pulls out, and the space between us is oddly quiet. I'm frozen, my brain struggling to catch up with what just happened.

Because Chancellor Liam Castle just came in my mouth, and I don't know how I should feel about it.

Irate?

Empowered?

Turned on?

Repulsed?

All I am is discombobulated. Eyes burning, I let go of my nipples and wipe the musky dampness of him from my lips.

"Did I satisfy you, Chancellor?" The bite in my tone is front and center, brave and bold.

Instead of taking issue with my attitude, he seems amused, mouth curving into a rogue grin as he pulls me to my feet. "Do you hear me complaining?"

"No," I whisper, cheeks aflame as I lower my gaze to his throat.

He lifts my chin. "Did you enjoy pleasuring me?"

"No!" The denial is too quick. He knows it. I know it.

That grin of his brightens. "Tell the truth, Novalee."

I nibble on my lower lip, hesitating. "It wasn't horrible."

He laughs. "Your honesty is refreshing."

"Do you generally inspire dishonesty in people, Chancellor?"

"It's *Liam*." His tone softens. "The woman I plan to marry will call me by my name. Is that understood?"

"Yes...Liam."

"That's better." His hands are still on me, a thumb brushing the pad of my abused lips, the slide of his fingers in my hair. Now that he's started touching me, he can't seem to stop.

And I can't find the strength to dislike it.

"To answer your question..." He lets a heavy beat pass. "People know better than to lie to me."

I don't know if he means it as a warning, but I take it as one.

Liam Castle is not someone you lie to.

He's not someone you disobey.

And he's definitely not someone you fall in love with.

"So tell me, Novalee Van Buren. Did you enjoy the taste of my cock?"

Cock.

Another word I'm familiar with, though there's an undercurrent of *wrong* stringing those letters together. It's bolder and filthier than erection or penis.

It's raw and filthy and...sexy.

"I...I don't know. It's the first time I ever tasted a man."

"It certainly won't be the last." Liam retrieves my clothing from the floor. "Selma will show you to your quarters."

"My quarters?" I shrug into my top and button the front.

"Yes, you'll have your own set of rooms on the penthouse floor. We'll share meals together, of course." After I'm once again decent, he takes my hand and pulls me toward the door of the library. "Did you not expect to have your own quarters?"

"I thought..." I trail off with a nervous swallow. Liam embodies the spirit of a man in control of his urges and desires, but he also seems like the type of man that wants you at his beck and call, available upon command. "I guess I thought you'd want me to share your bed."

Jerking me to a stop two feet from the door, he takes me by the chin in what I'm learning is his signature move. "My brothers might wish to share their bed with you, but I'm not a masochist."

I'm unprepared for the pang of hurt that goes off in my chest, and I respond before weighing my words. "You don't want me?"

"Who wouldn't want you, my sweet girl?" He dips his head, bringing our lips a few inches apart, and I breathe in his spicy scent. "But I know my limits when it comes to keeping you pure. Until you are crowned as *my* queen, I'll have my way with your mouth, but I won't have you in my bed."

3

The ride to the top of the tower is excruciatingly slow. I'm barely holding on to my composure. By the time Selma shows me to my private quarters, I'm full-on shaking. I dismiss the maid before scurrying inside, desperate for a moment alone so I can process what just happened on the first floor of this circular fortress.

I don't realize the hot mess of my face until Faye rushes to me, eyes wide with alarm.

"What did that bastard do to you?"

Her vehemence, her unwavering support—it makes me buckle on the spot. I sob into my hands, knees meeting the floor. I'm not even sure why I'm falling apart.

Because Liam Castle got under my skin with a single blow job? It makes little sense. All I know is I'm reeling, and I can't seem to stop.

"Novalee! Talk to us. What happened?"

"I don't know if I can do this." I stare at my ladies through the flood of tears escaping my eyes.

"Was he mean?" Elise asks, cautious hesitation sharp in the lines of her porcelain skin.

Faye is more direct. "Did he hurt you?" She narrows her brows, purses her lips with protective, ball-busting intent. "Because if he hurt you..."

She'll do nothing. We're women in a foreign place that doesn't afford us the same rights as men. They'll say we're weak and not as smart, but at the core of my heart, I know that's not true.

Because it takes true strength and wit to survive a group of men like the Zodiac Brotherhood. Especially with a man like Liam at their head.

"He didn't hurt me."

Faye stands in a fluid and graceful motion, though the harsh angles on her face are anything but. She helps me to my feet. "Are you sure?"

"I'm sure."

"But something *did* happen?" Faye never side-steps the blunt questions—the ones that drag you kicking and screaming to the center of the bullseye. I'm pinned there now, unwilling to share what happened with my ladies, but helpless to find a graceful way out of it.

"He made me..." I hold her gaze as Elise stiffens. The two of them are the closest I'll ever have to sisters, and we've talked about sex in the past, but the idea of confiding what Liam made me do, down to the last dirty detail, has my cheeks flaming.

Faye takes my hand. "You know you can tell us anything."

"He asked me to...go down on him." Though he didn't

ask, and I'm too ashamed to admit how powerless I was in the moment.

Faye raises a dark brow. "Did you enjoy it?"

"It didn't...completely...repulse me."

Elise exhales as if she'd been holding her breath for the last minute. "Don't tease us. What was it like?"

Internally, I cringe at her noticeable excitement, but that's Elise—always smiling and keeping things positive. From the day she came to live on our lands three years ago, she's always been a glass-half-full kind of girl. Though I've never had the experience of a broken heart, Elise would be the first to offer a pint of chocolate ice cream and a collection of chick flicks.

Faye would be too busy kicking the ass of the man who'd hurt me to join in on the movie marathon. Between the two of them, they have me covered. I dart my gaze between my closest friends, taking note of their expectant faces, hearing their mutual silent question.

What was it like pleasuring a man like Liam Castle?

Scary.

Exhilarating.

Rough.

Arousing.

Shameful.

"I need to prepare for dinner," I say, sidestepping the subject altogether.

Faye's sigh of exasperation disrupts the dark curl teasing her left eye. "Fine. We'll shelve this conversation for later." She wants to needle me for more info on the art of oral sex, but she doesn't. Instead, she turns to Elise. "Lay out a dress for the queen. I'll draw a bath."

"Something in black, please," I tell Elise as I follow Faye into the en suite bathroom. The color's appropriate for a rebellion, suitable for a funeral. The perfect camouflage to face twelve predatory men over dinner.

Several minutes later, I'm sinking into hot water with a relieved sigh, suds rising over my breasts. My nipples poke through the bubbles, over-sensitive from the change in temperature, and the chancellor plays on my mind like flashes on a picture reel.

The confidence in his touch.

The command in his voice.

The surrender on his face when he came.

A strong, foreign urge to touch myself ignites inside me. I glance at Faye, who's taken a seat at the vanity, waiting to offer her help should I need it.

What I need is privacy.

"I can dress on my own tonight for dinner. You and Elise should settle into your quarters and get ready."

Through narrowed eyes, she studies me as if searching for everything I'm not saying. "Are you sure you're okay?"

"I'm fine. I just need some time alone."

"Of course."

After she leaves me alone with my lustful thoughts, I waste no time in pushing a hand between my legs. I've never felt so decadent and sinful. Steam rises off my slick skin, and I close my eyes as my fingers explore, increasing the rhythm once I press on the spot that feels especially good. I let those stored pictures of Liam play in my head. Hear his voice in my ears. Pretend the touch of my fingers are his. I flush even hotter, my heartbeat pounding behind my breastbone.

I've never been so close. Instead of shying away, like I did the last time I touched myself, I increase the pressure and speed, imagining the chancellor bracing above me, bare chest grazing my nipples.

He unlocked something deep inside me when he used my mouth the way he did. Something naughty and primal. A yearning that wasn't there before—the need to know what it's like to surrender to oneself.

To surrender to someone else.

I push two fingertips inside my pussy and envision his cock there instead. "Liam," I moan, the plea for more rumbling off my lips.

And that's when someone sucks in a harsh breath.

My eyes flick open.

The man of my fantasies is standing at the foot of the tub, his toffee eyes reduced to slits. Both hands form fists at his sides.

I veer upright, hands covering my chest, and water sloshes everywhere. "What are you doing in here!"

"I live here."

"But these are my private quarters."

"You won't find a place on this island I don't have access to." He rounds the tub and hauls me out of the water to stand before him in stunned mortification. "Did you come?"

My cheeks flame even hotter. "N-no."

Water runs in rivulets down my skin, dripping from my hair, soaking the plush mat under my feet. Blood throbs between my legs, a wondrous itch I can't scratch. As displeasure darkens his beautiful features, I can't help but grieve for the climax that didn't happen. What would it have felt like to tip over the edge?

"Orgasm is a gift," he says, his grip tight on my wrist as he pulls me out of my suite of rooms and into the shared space of the penthouse. "You're never to take it without permission."

I'm shaking as he drags me into his quarters. The dip of the sun toward the horizon casts the space in shadow, and the heavy furnishings give an undertone of masculine virility. A bed designed for a king sits atop a platform in the middle of the room, outfitted in midnight blue. A color fit for royalty.

He ushers me away from the bed and gently shoves me into a seat at a small table in front of a set of French doors. Beyond the glass, I spy a balcony. "You're not to come in here unless I instruct otherwise. Do you understand?"

"Y-yes," I say, teeth chattering. "Why am I here?"

"Lay your hands on the table, palms up."

I obey, knowing now is not the time to question him. With a decisive nod, he strides across the room and pulls something down from a rack on the wall. My stomach drops upon his return.

"Do you know what this is?"

A hard swallow precedes my answer. "It's a riding crop."

"Do you know why your hands are on that table right now?"

Without thinking, I yank them back.

"Do not move them." The leather end of the crop makes a harsh smack on the table, punctuating his command.

I inch my hands back into position, every fiber of my being urging to me to take flight. But how far would I get?

Out of this room? Maybe I'd breach the penthouse door before he catches up with me. Maybe I'd make it into the elevator, then I could streak through the tower as naked as the day I was born.

"Do you understand why you're being punished?"

"Because I was touching myself?"

"Because you did it without permission."

"You're not being fair. I didn't know it was against the rules."

"Discipline is how you learn, Novalee." He gestures to my vulnerable, exposed palms. "If you move your hands again, I'll have no choice but to take you to our enforcer for punishment. Trust me, neither of us wants that."

His threat collides inside me, a fatal crash of anger and fear. Trust him, he says. I want to laugh and cry and scream at the irony in that demand. As he steps back and raises the crop, an ominous preamble, I remind myself that I've been through worse.

I needed medical attention and a soft cushion for a week after Uncle Rowan unleashed his whip on my backside for trying to escape.

"You'll receive five strikes to each palm." His hand twitches, a millisecond away from inflicting pain, and our eyes lock. "Brace yourself, my sweet girl."

Smack!

I jump, suck in a breath, and another notch of anger forms on my armor. He brings the crop down on my left palm.

Then the right.

Back and forth, reddening my fair skin.

Causing my eyes to water.

I glare at him through my unshed tears.

Before the fifth and final set, he stops to take a deep breath, and my arms quake on the table, hands burning from his abuse. My soul brims with rage, but underneath that, I'm hurt. I hate that my heart throbs with the traitorous emotion, throat aching from the toll of holding it back.

Because I thought he was different, believing we had a connection despite the reality of our power exchange. Did he not feel it too, back in the library with his cum still lingering on my lips?

He issues the last two strikes, making them count, and my teeth grind from the intensity of the sting. My toes curl with it, muscles stiff.

I don't dare move my hands.

I don't move at all.

"It's over." He sounds relieved, which is ludicrous because he wasn't the one suffering a physical punishment. Setting the crop aside, he pulls me to my feet. "I'm not a sadist," he says, sliding his hand along my cheek. "I don't enjoy inflicting pain."

"You get off on the control."

The corners of his mouth twitch. A hint of a smile? A scowl? He's so hard to read. "That's probably true, but next time you'll think twice before touching what's mine."

His words slide over me like a physical caress, and I clench my thighs in response. The hue of his gaze deepens to raw umber.

I swear he knows the effect he has on me.

"I believe you when you say you didn't come." His

thumb traces the outline of my lips. "Your skin is flushed with the need to orgasm." He sends a cursory glance at my chest. "And your nipples are begging for my mouth."

A whimper escapes onto the soft pad of his thumb. I can't resist darting my tongue out to taste him.

"Jesus, must you test my control?" He pushes his thumb into my mouth, and I suck on it, reminiscent of the way I serviced his manhood. "So innocent, but so responsive. You're an anomaly, a vibrant orchid in the dead of winter." He dips his thumb into my mouth three times, playing on my tongue before withdrawing. "Do you touch yourself often?"

"No."

His nostrils flare. "Have you ever had an orgasm?"

"What do you think, Chancellor?"

"I think you're going to end up over my lap for refusing to use my name."

That mental image doesn't inspire fear in me as it should. "I don't mean to disobey you."

"Then answer the question."

"I've never had an orgasm."

"You're very responsive for a woman who never learned to pleasure herself."

"I tried once."

"Did you not enjoy yourself? Because you seemed to enjoy yourself just fine in my bathtub."

"It felt awkward then." I lower my gaze. "Today, it didn't."

Today, I had the memory of blowing him as inspiration.

"You're not to pleasure yourself without my permission again," he says, gripping me by the chin. "Is that clear?"

His command shivers through my bones. "Yes."

"Your first orgasm belongs to me. Your pussy is off-limits to your fingers until I decide to give that gift to you."

For the first time since I learned of my fate six years ago, I experience a thrilling sense of anticipation.

4

After dressing for dinner, we arrive on the first floor. The silk skirt of my black dress swishes against my legs as Liam takes me by the elbow and leads me down a wide hallway. I'm entranced by the huge portraits on either side, gawking wide-eyed at the larger-than-life forms of what I assume are the Brotherhood's ancestors.

"Can I ask you something?"

"Of course."

"How did the Zodiac Brotherhood begin?"

He stalls in the middle of the hall, attention on the portrait that has captured me so.

"That's Evangeline Castle. She was my grandmother by several degrees of greatness. And I mean that in every sense of the word." Letting go of my arm, he tangles his fingers with mine, and I hide a wince because my palms are still tender from his punishment. "She was only eighteen when she set sail with a group of explorers. They would have never discovered the island without her unusual skills."

"Unusual?"

He nods toward the portrait of his ancestor. "She knew the nighttime sky better than most men. The constellations and planets, and their position depending on the season. At first, the explorers believed she was a superstitious soul, but after she predicted two potential catastrophes, they started listening to her." He sends a cursory glance down the hall. "She led them here, and by doing so, they escaped certain death in a storm. Got rich in the process too, because the island was uninhabited and abundant with gold."

He wanders down the hall a few paces, pulling me along until we're staring at a portrayal of a group of men from what appears to be the 17th century. "Are these men the explorers?"

"Yes. Evangeline was a progressive thinker. An Amelia Earhart of her time. But they couldn't deny there was something special about her." He tilts his head, and our gazes lock. "There were twelve explorers, one for each zodiac sign."

"That's quite a coincidence."

"We don't believe in coincidences, Novalee. The explorers didn't either. Evangeline became their prized queen, shared among the twelve but locked away in a tower."

"Why did they lock her up?"

"She wanted to leave the island. They didn't."

"So she was their prisoner?" Sickness rises in my gut at the thought.

"Their prisoner, their queen, and the mother of their children."

I gape at him, my mind spinning through the implications of what he just said. "She's not just *your* ancestor, is she?"

"No. All twelve of us are descendants of Evangeline Castle."

"But you bear her surname."

"She took the last name of the explorer born under Aries. Legend has it she favored him the most."

"So you're telling me this entire island was founded and bred from one woman? What about incest?"

"Evangeline's direct descendants have always brought in outsiders to marry. It's tradition, just as it's tradition to compete for a queen's hand in marriage at the start of a new Brotherhood."

"And how is the new Brotherhood chosen?"

His lips curve into a grin. "You're full of questions, aren't you, my sweet girl?"

"I'm just trying to understand it all." Slowly, we move down the hall once more.

"The Brotherhood shifts power every twenty-five years or so. Each house bears the duty of producing a male heir born under its zodiac sign. Once all twelve heirs come of age, the tradition renews, and a new virgin queen is found." He gives me the side-eye. "This is privileged information."

"It sounds like a tradition based on superstition."

"Men have tested the tradition over the years. The outcomes were never good."

"How so?"

"Disease and death, mostly. When we follow tradition, we prosper. When we don't…"

A shiver takes hold of me. Or was that an actual cold draft hitting my back? Suddenly, I wish I'd chosen a dress that wasn't backless—or at least left my hair down. Gooseflesh erupts on my skin.

"Why is the queen always a virgin? Evangeline wasn't a virgin to all twelve."

"She was a virgin to only one."

"Which one?"

A shadow seems to cross his face. "The House of Leo."

I'm curious about his issue with Leo, but I don't want to risk shutting down this conversation. We take a few more steps toward the open doors leading into the dining room, and I wait for the furrow between his dark brows to disappear before asking my next question. "What happens if one of the houses can't produce an heir?"

"If fertility issues arise, we do whatever is necessary to produce an heir. Surrogates have been used in the past. So have mistresses."

Something close to possessiveness rushes up inside me, and I imagine the man I'm to marry in bed with another woman. I don't like that idea at all. And I don't like that the man in my hypothetical vision is Liam. I've only known him for a day, but I'm becoming...attached.

How will I navigate the next twelve months without crushing my heart in the process? The potential for total annihilation is too great. No matter the outcome, someone will get hurt.

Several someones.

"What if a member of the Brotherhood is the one with the fertility problem?"

Liam stops, and the look he gives me is so intense, I'm tempted to take a step back. "That's never happened, Novalee."

"That's...improbable at best and impossible at most."

"The tradition hasn't let us down yet."

He urges me forward, and we arrive at the entrance of the formal dining room where my ladies are waiting. As Faye greets Liam with an air of coldness degrees below her usual aloofness, I suddenly remember my conversation with her before my bath.

The bath.

The one he interrupted and punished me for.

How could I forget, even for a moment, how absolute his power is? He pulled me in with his history lesson in the hall, seducing me with the mystery of the Brotherhood's origins. Liam stimulates my mind as much as he stimulates my body.

What a dangerous combination.

"Ready to go in, ladies?" Liam gestures for us to enter first. I step into the elaborate dining room, my ladies on either side of me, and take in the circular space. Above a giant round table hangs a massive chandelier. There are no windows in this room, as we're deep in the middle of the tower on the first floor.

It's a stifling place, especially with eleven sets of eyes gawking at me from their thrones around the table.

Liam moves us forward, and I realize the table is sectioned into twelve slices. He clears his throat. "I'm pleased to present our queen, Novalee Van Buren and her ladies, Faye and Elise."

I bow my head in a show of respect. Liam gestures for me to take a seat, then he settles into the chair on my right as my ladies sit on my left. We're all connected at this table —a continuous circle that never ends.

"Before we make formal introductions," Liam says, "I'd like to present Novalee with a gift." He waves a hand at Selma, who crosses to the table carrying a tray with a white round box. Liam picks it up and opens the top before setting it on the table.

A humongous diamond ring glitters under the light of the chandelier.

His brown eyes are warm, and there's a hint of a smile on his lips as he takes my left hand in his. "Every member of the Brotherhood will present you with a gift at the beginning of his time with you. This ring is mine. It symbolizes the Brotherhood's commitment to you and your duty to us."

He slides it onto my ring finger, and I can't help but gawk at the brilliance of the stone. It's beautiful and weighs down my hand as much as the next twelve months weigh on my shoulders.

But I've recently learned that beautiful things come with hard realities.

"It's stunning," I whisper.

"So are you." He raises my hand to his lips, the one he just put a ring on—the one he punished earlier that evening—and places a kiss there.

And he says I'm an anomaly.

Liam is a contradiction of harsh and tender.

"Gentlemen," he says, facing the men at the table, "please stand and announce yourselves in the order of your houses."

The man sitting on the other side of Faye rises. His dark hair is cropped close to his head, the line of his nose aristocratic.

"Heath, House of Taurus."

There's a stoicism about him that makes me uncomfortable, and I'm already dreading the following month with him.

The next man in the circle stands, and I narrow my eyes as I try to recall how I know him. Technically, I met all twelve of these men six years ago, but this man—with his emerald eyes and easy-going smile—seems especially familiar.

"Landon, House of Gemini."

Then his smile widens, and I remember. He was the eldest of the twelve, and he *laughed* at me, taken aback by my young age. He still seems to laugh at me, eyes twinkling in some private joke of which I'm not partial.

A man with a blond ponytail takes the floor next. "Vance, House of Cancer." His smile isn't as inviting as Landon's, but I sense a gentleness in him that puts me at ease. Vance reclaims his seat, and my attention lands on the man next to him.

His blond hair sticks out in careless abandon, and his rumpled clothes make me think he fell out of bed and threw on the first pair of jeans he found. There's an air of haughty boredom about him as he rises to his feet.

I'm taken aback by the hostility in his blue eyes. They bore into me, and I remember the way he taunted me the first time I met him.

"Sebastian, House of Leo."

The lion. I should have known. I expect him to settle into his seat again now that he's introduced himself, but he doesn't.

"How do we know she hasn't spread her legs already?" the lion asks, directing the question at the chancellor, though his obvious distaste of my existence shreds to the soul. My jaw hangs open, and I'm about to object when Liam squeezes my knee in a silent command to stay quiet.

"Watch your mouth, Sebastian. The queen has done nothing to earn your scorn. She deserves your *respect*."

"Respect is earned. Isn't that what our fathers always told us?"

"I'm done with this conversation."

"But you never answered my question, *Chancellor*. Just because her uncle promised us a virgin doesn't mean she hasn't fucked half the male population of her nation."

Liam slams a fist onto the table. "Enough!"

Vance clears his throat. "Tomorrow, I'll examine her to confirm virginity."

"And what about her willingness to cooperate?" Sebastian says. "I have no interest in babysitting a brat."

The rage wafting off Liam is tangible. "Her obedience has been tested."

"I need my own reassurances." Even as he says the words, I sense Sebastian is only trying to provoke the chancellor.

"Then you'll get your damn reassurances," Liam snaps. "Tomorrow, during the examination, you'll all have the chance to confirm her virginity and test her willingness. Satisfied?"

Sebastian smirks. "For now." He settles into his chair with a vibe of smugness that pokes at my indignation.

I'm barely present, my mind spinning in righteous anger at the man whose aqua gaze is still burning a hole through my armor.

A chair scrapes the floor, and a voice startles me to

attention. "Let's get back to the introductions, shall we? I'm Miles, House of Virgo."

Then the next stands. "Pax, House of Libra."

One by one, the remaining members of the Brotherhood arise and announce their names and zodiac signs...as if I'll remember them all after the argument that just took place.

As if I can concentrate on anything but the festering hatred of the man sitting six seats to my left.

Determined to do just that, I force my gaze on each man as he stands, studiously ignoring the lion and his display of contempt.

"Ford, House of Scorpio."

"Tatum, House of Sagittarius."

The houses of Capricorn, Aquarius, and Pisces close out the round of introductions.

Oliver.

Hugo.

Sullivan.

Twelve gorgeous men, dressed in everything from expensive Armani to Levi denim, and at this overbearing roundtable of testosterone and power, only one other thing besides the zodiac unites them.

Me.

5

"Time to arise! The sun is shining, and it's a warm day."
Movement draws my eyes open, and I find Selma parting the floor-length drapes, allowing the light of day to spill into the room. I hide my face in the soft pillow with a groan.

"Did you not sleep well?" she asks.

"Not really." What an understatement. After Liam escorted me to my suite last night, pressing his lips to my forehead in a brief kiss goodnight, I tossed and turned for hours, my mind galloping ahead with memories of my first day on Zodiac Island.

Liam's confident control.

Sebastian's casual cruelty.

"Chancellor Castle is expecting you on the main balcony in twenty minutes."

I veer up in bed too fast, making my head woozy from the rush of blood. Selma enters the adjacent closet that's bigger than most people's bedrooms, and I spy my clothing hanging on racks and taking up the space on the shelves.

She slides several hangers to the side, apparently searching for something specific.

"Where are my ladies? They usually help me dress."

"The chancellor wishes not to be disturbed today. He gave them the day off from their duties."

I slide out of bed and frown, not liking his high-handedness. Selma exits the wardrobe room, clutching a white negligee that leaves little to the imagination. That scrap of material definitely didn't come with me to the island.

"Chancellor Castle wants you to wear this to breakfast." She drapes it over the back of a burgundy lounge chair, the dark suede leather offering a stark contrast to the purity of white.

"And if I don't?"

"Well, that's your choice, but just know the chancellor doesn't let disobedience go unpunished."

I fist my hands, remembering the sting that disappeared overnight during my fitful sleep, though the phantom of the burn lingers.

As Selma makes my bed, I grab the piece of lingerie and escape into the bathroom.

Several minutes later, after a solitary pep talk, I stand in front of the full-length mirror with my dusty rose nipples on display in the fitted lace cups. The skirt flares down to my knees, giving a false sense of modesty because the material is sheer, and underneath I'm wearing a thong. My long hair is my only option for modesty, so I arrange it over my shoulders to cover my breasts.

When I return to the bedroom, teeth freshly brushed and bladder emptied, I find the room deserted and as clean as it was upon my arrival yesterday. The curved outer wall is a wondrous panel of oversized windows that reveal a breathtaking view of the sea, and just like in Liam's quarters, a set of French doors opens to a balcony.

I wander to the glass, brushing my fingers against the spotless surface, and wish I could stay inside this private sanctuary all day, safe from the lustful attention of a man who makes me feel shameful things.

But a glance at the clock startles me into motion. I spent more time in the bathroom than I realized, and now I'm already ten minutes late.

This isn't good.

It's the only thought bouncing around my head as I rush through my private sitting room and into the main part of the penthouse. The scent of food—a mixture of cinnamon and sausage—wafts through the open doors of the balcony where I find him sitting alone at a table.

"I assume Selma told you twenty minutes?" He doesn't look at me as he asks the question, and the nature of his nonchalant tone makes me nervous.

I'm tempted to lie, but I don't have it in me. Not with him. "I'm sorry. I lost track of time in the bathroom."

He finally raises his head, his brown eyes a rich caramel from the warm sunlight. A slight breeze disturbs my hair, causing my nipples to poke through the strands. His attention lowers to my chest, and a furrow forms between his brows. Scooting his chair back, he picks up a wooden serving spoon from the table, and I stiffen, assuming he's going to use it to punish me. Instead, he uses the thin handle to secure my hair into a messy bun atop my head.

"Bend over the table," he says, gesturing to the end free of breakfast clutter. When I don't move to follow his command, he takes me by the elbow and leads me to where he wants me, and I feel him behind me as I splay my hands on the smooth surface. My breasts smash against the wood.

"Why are you doing this?"

"I have zero tolerance for tardiness." His shoe nudges the inside of my foot. "Spread your legs."

"What are you going to do to me?" I ask, voice shaking as I widen my stance.

"Not what I'd like to do." His fingers graze the back of my thigh, and slowly he lifts the skirt, bearing my ass cheeks to the temperate spring air. "If you were mine to fuck, I'd take you right here on this table." He pauses, and I sense the heat of his gaze on me, spreading gooseflesh down my back.

I shiver, though whether from the mild temperature or Liam's words, I don't know.

"If you were mine," he says, pressing into my back as he brings his lips to my ear, "I'd get you worked up enough to beg, but I wouldn't let you come." He tucks the skirt around my waist, leaving my backside vulnerable to his every whim.

I swallow hard. "I won't be late again."

"When I say twenty minutes, I mean twenty minutes. Understand?"

"Yes."

"Since you're still learning your boundaries, I won't use my belt this time, but you're getting a swat for every minute you were late."

The idea of his hand on my ass turns my insides to molten desire. "A total of ten?"

"Eleven, Novalee." His warm palm settles on my right

cheek, fingers squeezing the flesh there. "But I wonder, my sweet girl, will my hand punish, or will it turn you on?"

I'm already turned on, but hell will ice over before I tell him that.

His palm lifts from my ass, and a second later, he lands a sound smack. I jump, unable to hold back a yelp because his hand hurts more than I thought it would. He lands another, and another, each one escalating in force. Gnawing on my lower lip, I fist my hands against the table, hoping to find the strength to get through the last half of the spanking.

His hand comes down again, and I can't help but cry out. "You're hurting me."

"Yes. That *is* the idea behind a corporal punishment."

"But it was only ten minutes!"

"It was eleven."

Whack!

A pitiful whimper escapes my lips. I never knew a spanking could be so painful, could humiliate to this degree. My face burns, undoubtedly as red as my ass.

He issues the last strike—an especially harsh blow of his hand—and then he makes me sit on my hands at the table.

"Now you'll wait eleven minutes before you eat." He reclaims his seat and casually lifts his coffee cup to his lips.

"Why are you so cruel?" He's better than this, better than Sebastian and his caustic personality. I've seen it.

Liam meets my angry gaze, and I think I detect an apology there; one he doesn't want to give voice to.

"What you call cruelty, I call consistency. As the first in this tower to spend time with you, it's my job to make sure you know your boundaries." He pauses, and a beat passes, laden with importance. "I'm not being cruel, Novalee. I'm arming you against those who will take discipline and control to Draconian levels."

Fear flourishes in my gut, unstoppable. It's a weed I can't control. An invasive sickness I can't cure.

"You're scaring me," I whisper past the aching lump in my throat.

"I'm scared *for* you."

"Why?" I ask, running through the events of the previous day, and the introductions at dinner. "Is it Sebastian? Is he dangerous?"

"Sebastian should be the least of your worries, my sweet girl."

"Then who should I be worried about?"

"Truthfully? All of us, myself included." He blinks, and something close to hesitation crosses his face. "I'll do my best to prepare you, but I can't protect you after you leave my house."

"Why not? Aren't you the chancellor?"

"My power only goes so far. Every man in this tower will have authority over you until the auction."

"But I get no say in who I marry, isn't that right, *Chancellor?*" The title slips out, as does the testy note in my tone. I don't apologize for it, or take it back—I'm too angry at the situation that's been forced upon me.

He grips me by the arm and hoists me out of the chair. "Is your ass not red enough, my queen?"

His threat does little to put me in my place, which is where he wants me. I'm too busy recalling the warmth of his hand on my backside. His punishment was painful, but the memory of it doesn't overshadow the way this man makes me feel when he puts his hands on me.

"You don't scare me, Liam Castle."

"That makes one of us." He releases my arm, and the warmth in his eyes deepens as he pulls the impromptu hair stick from my bun. My blond locks cascade around my shoulders, free for the tangle of his fingers.

"How do *I* scare *you?*" It's a preposterous concept that this strong, confident man fears me.

"You behold more power than you realize." His breath dances on my lips, suddenly quick and shallow. Three eternal seconds pass, heavy with mutual yearning.

Then he slams his mouth on mine with a groan. A gasp escapes me as I part my lips for his insistent tongue. His kiss, deep and consuming, sears me to my soul. I whimper into his mouth, fingers clutching his suit jacket as heat ignites between my legs.

I've never been kissed until now. Have never known what it means to burn for a man until Liam lit the match.

He groans again, and I reciprocate his vow of surrender. He lifts me onto the table amid rattling china and settles between my thighs. His hands are in my hair, his hot, open mouth devouring the column of my throat, cock hard and snug against the wet center of my innocence.

I don't feel innocent anymore. I'm wanton with sin, wrecked by lust. An accusing pang attacks my heart because I'm not being honest with myself.

Lust could turn into more.

I could grow to love him, and that scares me more than anything he could do to me on a physical level.

He yanks the sheer cups of the negligee down, and his thumbs brush over my nipples. "Touch yourself like you did in the tub yesterday."

"You're giving me permission?"

"To touch, yes." He veers back and holds me captive in his stare. "Not to come." He pushes my hand between us, urging me to dip my fingers beneath the barrier of scant panties.

A moan slips free, and our eyes lock as I grip his shoulder. His are beautiful, sensual and deep, surrounded by thick lashes. The way he watches me makes my breath stall.

"Are you wet for me?" His hand covers mine, adding pressure to that magical spot I found yesterday, alone in the tub.

"Yes."

Our hands move in tandem, creating an exquisite fire-inducing friction. The kind of friction that has me breathless and unable to stop.

"Liam." His name fights its way through the vise around my throat.

"Say it again," he whispers.

I groan his name as I graze the pinnacle, and that's when he yanks my hand out of my panties, leaving me throbbing as blood rushes toward the dam.

"Please," I beg, delirious and floating in a foreign headspace. I try returning my hand back to the center of all that pressure and heat, but he won't let me. I'm breathing too hard as he brings each of my fingers into his mouth.

He's *tasting* me.

Making me whimper with each dart of his tongue.

Shooting pulsating need to every nerve ending in my body.

"Please," I say again, voice a quivering sigh.

"Begging won't get you what you want."

"Then what will?"

"Patience." His answer splashes ice on my flushed skin.

"Do you enjoy torturing me?"

"If it makes you ache for my cock, then yes. I enjoy torturing you." He steps back, and I slide to my feet. "Hurry and eat your cold breakfast. We can't be late for your medical examination."

6

The room is large yet claustrophobic, made up of four windowless walls. Several paintings of the sea are on display, and the cabinetry is made from distressed wood—a sandy tone that complements the ocean theme. The decor is designed to evoke an informal vibe, to soothe and calm, but that's impossible because twelve chairs form a circle around the examination bench.

Liam urges me forward. "We don't have much time before everyone arrives." We stall in front of the bench, and he slides his palm along my cheek. "I wish this was just a medical exam, but it's much more than that. My brothers will touch you, Novalee."

"Please don't let this happen." Not like this, in front of him with the memory of his kiss fresh in my mind.

"I need you to cooperate. Things will go quicker and smoother if you do." His thumb inches toward the corner of my mouth. "That also holds true for the months after you leave me."

An entire year of this, followed by a lifetime of servitude to the man who wins my hand in marriage. If the man is someone like Liam—kind and just no matter the punishment he unleashes—the marriage might not be too horrible.

But if someone like Sebastian wins the auction...

I shiver at the thought.

Liam takes a step back and gestures at the ankle-length skirt I chose to wear. "Undress from the waist down."

A ball of sickness lands in my gut. Losing my modesty in front of him was hard enough; undressing for twelve sets of eyes is unfathomable. I pull the waistband down my legs and step out of the material. I'm not wearing panties since he told me not to.

He picks up my skirt and hangs it on a hook on the wall. "Hop up."

Bracing my hands on the bench, I lift my ass onto the leather, legs dangling over the edge. "Do all twelve of you share dinner every night?"

"No. Last night's dinner was in your honor. We'll hold a dinner at the start of each new month for you."

Another tradition.

But I'm glad I won't have to face them every day.

The door opens behind me, sending a wave of dread down my backside. It chills me from the crown of my head to the soles of my feet, and my skin pebbles with gooseflesh. Liam takes a seat on my left. I bow my head, and from the corner of my eye, I spy the members of the Brotherhood filing in and settling into the chairs surrounding me.

When I raise my eyes, I find Sebastian staring back. His eyes are the most alarming shade of blue I've ever seen—a brilliant azure. He's brazen in the way he's watching me.

I press my naked thighs together, clinging to my last thread of modesty. Because there's no escaping his scrutiny. My skin flushes, chasing away the chill in my bones.

Next, I steal a glance at Liam, but his attention fixates on Sebastian, eyes dark and shooting daggers—a cocktail of jealous anger. The chair to the left of Sebastian remains empty. Instead, the doctor—from the house of Cancer—halts in front of me without preamble.

"Lie back," he orders.

I do as I'm told, fitting my feet into the stirrups he pulls out, and a whisper of air caresses my inner thighs, bringing about a violent shudder. Driven by modesty and instinct, I bring my knees together.

"Knees apart. I can't examine you otherwise."

I hesitate too long, and he pries them open, putting me on display for half the room to ogle. I study the ceiling as shame burns my throat. No one's ever looked at me down there, let alone touched me.

Not even the family doctor.

Not even Liam when he pressed his hand over mine during breakfast.

"Teresa, come over here, love," the doctor orders a maid standing in my periphery. "The queen could use your hand."

"Yes, Master Vance."

I keep my gaze trained on the ceiling as footsteps scurry to my side. A warm hand enfolds mine, fingers squeezing in silent support.

"This won't take long," Vance says as he settles between my knees. At the first touch of his fingers spreading my nether lips, I grit my teeth. Teresa gives my hand another squeeze, sensing my discomfort, and I think we both hold our breath as the doctor gently pushes a finger inside me.

I wish I had a clock to watch, hands counting down each excruciating second, or even a speck on the ceiling to focus on as Vance violates my insides. But there's no escaping this. I bite my lip as my feet tremble in the stirrups. The man is a doctor, and I'm aware that women go through this every day, but considering the circumstances, I feel utterly violated.

I didn't ask for this. I didn't even give my permission.

"Almost done," Teresa says.

My head lolls to the side, and unbidden, I find Sebastian. His jaw is an unshaven line in a face cast from strength and sensuality. But those azure eyes...

They burn right through me. Or maybe they're burning for me.

As we lock gazes, his nostrils flare. A tick goes off in his jaw. I wish I had a decoder for this man—this silent man whose stare somehow tells me more than words can give away.

There's more to him than disdain and anger.

He. Wants. Me.

The realization plays on the heightened air between us, and the spell isn't broken until Vance finishes the exam.

"The hymen is fully intact." He pushes off on his chair, wheels rolling across the gleaming marble as he waves a hand in Liam's direction. "Chancellor, the floor is yours."

Teresa lets go of my hand and disappears into the periphery, her stance by the door becoming that of an unobtrusive spectator.

I suck in a breath and hold it as Liam settles between

my thighs. Keeping his gaze averted, he inserts a finger into me, and it's the first time he's touched me like this. I despise that he's doing so under the watchful attention of eleven other men.

His face is carved from granite, and I sense the control he's holding on to. Without ceremony, he withdraws his hand and steps back before gesturing for Heath to go next. "Proceed."

Heath barely touches me at all. He doesn't offer me more than a passing glance either.

Landon, from the House of Gemini, breaks the ice first. "You were young all those years ago, and I won't lie. I was skeptical, but you've matured, haven't you, Novalee?" His tone is conversational. Not surprising for a Gemini, I suppose.

"I have."

"Do you mind if I touch you?"

"Do I have a choice?"

"You have a valid point, my queen. I'd still like your permission."

"I can't in good conscience give it, but you have my dubious cooperation."

"You are a feisty little spitfire, I'll give you that," he says with a laugh. "I'll have to take your word and the testimony of my brothers as proof of your purity." He reclaims his seat, and Sebastian stands, the next in line since Vance was the first to test my virginity during the exam.

"You heard the queen," Sebastian says with a smirk. "Her cooperation is questionable. I want her restrained."

Liam scowls. "That's not necessary."

"I think it is." Sebastian snaps his fingers at Teresa. "Fetch me a set of wrist and ankle cuffs from the dungeon."

I shoot a startled look at Liam. "There's a dungeon?"

He winces. "I was hoping to spare you from that information until later."

"Why is there a dungeon?" The question shrieks through the room.

"It exists for pleasure," Liam says.

"Don't coddle her." The man I remember only as Libra snickers. "The dungeon is primarily for punishment, so keep that in mind, my queen, lest you end up in my hands."

I'm close to having a panic attack by the time Teresa returns with a set of leather cuffs. Sebastian wastes no time is fastening my wrists and ankles to the bench legs. He tests the anchors holding me captive, then he circles me, just like he did all those years ago.

"If you're the merchandise, and I'm a prospective buyer, I think a little due diligence is in order." He stalls by my head, his smirk tangling with Liam's deepening scowl.

I can almost taste the animosity between them, and suddenly, I know this isn't about me. These two have unresolved issues, and I'm the pawn standing between them.

"Open your mouth, princess."

"What are you doing?" Liam growls.

"Exercising due diligence. If she becomes my wife, I'll require great head every morning."

"I assure you, her oral skills are top-notch," Liam says through clenched teeth.

"Your assurances mean shit to me." Sebastian brushes his thumb across my lips. "Open."

I do, and he thrusts his fingers inside my mouth until his knuckles hit my teeth, making me heave relentlessly.

"That'll be a tight fit for my cock."

I bite down on his fingers, and he yanks them out of my mouth. "Sounds to me like you're overestimating size," I say, glaring at him.

Someone laughs.

Sebastian isn't amused. "Good luck finding a woman with that complaint." He wanders to the end of the bench and stands between my spread legs. "Is your cunt as tight and pure as you claim?"

"Why don't you violate me and find out," I snap, tone dripping with scorn.

Someone laughs again. "She's got an attitude, that one."

I don't know who's finding amusement at my expense, because I haven't torn my eyes from Sebastian's. As he reaches between my thighs, pushing two fingers against the tight resistance of my innocence, his sea-blue gaze ignites.

My chest rises with a gasp, and I bite my lip when he presses his thumb on my clit. Out of all the hands that have invaded my innocence today, his is the one to drag a reaction from me. I pulse around his fingers, my body flooding with warmth and begging for his touch to go deeper.

To break past the barrier of purity and claim me.

He rubs circles on my throbbing nub, and I'm horrified by the moan that bleeds off my lips.

"That's enough!" Liam's voice thunders through the room.

I startle from the sound, but Sebastian doesn't react at all, other than to withdraw his fingers and stalk away, out of sight.

But not out of mind.

I listen to the thud of his retreating footfalls, followed by the slam of a door.

He just left.

Without a word.

Without a second thought.

Because I'm inconsequential to him. Someone he likes to toy with to get a rise out of his rival. His touch lit me on fire, but he felt nothing.

"Does anyone else need to continue with this charade?" Liam's voice reverberates through the room, a possessive warning to back off.

"No, Chancellor. I think we've seen enough." Landon leaves the room first, and one by one, the others follow. I let out a breath of relief as the door closes behind the last member of the Brotherhood.

Liam remains quiet as he unfastens the restraints. He hands my skirt to me, and I dress as the tension between us grows.

"Are you upset with me?" I ask, wishing I could wipe away the wetness between my legs.

Wipe away the evidence, erase the memory of Sebastian's touch.

"Why would I be upset with you?"

Heat flushes my face, and I can't meet his eyes. "Because of my reaction when Sebastian touched me."

"You can't help how your body responds, Novalee."

"But you seem angry."

"I'm angry at myself." He rakes a hand through his copper hair, disrupting the perfection. "I shouldn't have allowed this to happen."

"You said it yourself—you can't protect me."

"I can't protect you from my brothers, but I can protect us both from getting too emotionally involved."

"What do you mean?"

"What happened on the balcony today?" He pauses, and the air thickens with the memory of our kiss. "It can't happen again."

"You don't want me?"

"We already went over this. My attraction to you isn't in question. But I'm not the only one who wants you."

"I know the number of men who want to marry me. That doesn't mean they want *me*."

They only want a queen to fulfill the tradition. A conquest.

"One does." He takes me by the chin, a tender edge to his touch. "And by the way you looked at him, I know the attraction is mutual."

7

Sixteen days. Sixteen agonizingly long days that somehow pass too quickly. I spend the majority of them hiding in the penthouse, afraid of running into someone who *isn't* Liam. But I can't escape the irony, because Liam's been avoiding me the way I've been avoiding Sebastian.

We barely see each other, except for meals. Those we share, minus the skimpy lingerie.

And he doesn't touch me.

At all.

I know he wants to.

"This is fantastic," Faye says, studying my hasty sketch of an evening gown. The dress is backless with a mermaid skirt, and though it's done in charcoal, I envision a midnight blue, like the bedding in Liam's quarters.

"It's okay." I grasp a pencil and start on another sketch. "The skirt could use more flare."

"I think it's perfect." Faye sets the drawing on top of the others. "Elise would say the same thing."

Elise is touring the island with a prospective suitor, and Faye and I are sprawled on two lounge chairs in the main sitting room. Just because Liam has locked himself away in his quarters doesn't mean I have to.

And if I'm honest with myself, maybe I'm hoping to see him since a meeting at Zodiac Headquarters detained him all morning. He's been in his office ever since he came back, clinging to the distance growing between us.

"You're too critical of yourself," Faye says. "You could start a clothing line with these."

It's a subject we've talked about before. No doubt, it'll arise again because Faye is loyal and supportive. Bold and opinionated. Where I capitulate, she forges ahead, refusing to let anyone stand in her way.

She wants the same for me, as one of my ladies and a lifelong friend.

"She's right," Liam says, his deep voice startling me. I drop my pencil and turn around to find him standing in the archway that leads into the formal dining room. He saunters to the table and picks up a drawing. "You've got natural talent. You should pursue it."

"Maybe I would if the twelve of you weren't passing me around."

Faye gasps. "Novalee..."

She's not used to hearing me disrespect someone of authority. I'm not used to it, either.

Liam frowns. "I need to see you in my quarters." Without another word, he turns on his heel and leaves.

I push up from the lounge. "We'll continue this another time."

"Is he going to hurt you?"

"No."

"Are you sure?" Uncertainty lines her face.

I hide my own apprehension because I'm not sure what to expect from Liam. We've existed in this penthouse for the last couple of weeks by exchanging curt, polite conversation. But there's more between us—so much more—and the knowledge has only festered.

Now he's demanded my presence in his private quarters, and I don't know whether I'm elated or intimidated.

"It's okay, Faye. You should take the afternoon."

I exit the sitting room before she can object, but when I reach the heavy door blocking my entrance to the place where he sleeps, I stall, fist poised to knock.

Is he going to spank me again for my attitude?

Use his belt this time?

The latter causes my stomach to cramp.

I'm not ready to discover the harsher side of Liam.

I don't have a choice. Something has to give because he can't kiss me the way he did then ignore me the entire month of my stay in his house. I rap on the wood, my knuckles hitting harder than I intended. He flings the door open, and I slip past him, entering his formidable domain.

"Do you know how to play chess?"

His question catches me off-guard, and I whirl to face him, eyes wide in disbelief. "Chess, as in the *game*?"

A smile quirks on his lips. "Yes."

"I thought you called me in here to punish me."

"Oh, I did."

"I don't understand."

"Answer the question. Do you play?"

"Yes." Not very well, but I don't divulge that information. He's already got enough advantage on me.

"Shall we?" He gestures toward the table in front of the French doors where a game of chess awaits. As we each settle into a seat across from the other, I study him, trying to figure out what his true game is.

Because there's no way it's chess.

Since I'm sitting on the side with the white pieces, I take the first turn by moving a pawn forward two squares. "Your move, Chancellor."

He brings a pawn forward. "You're craving my hand today, aren't you, my sweet girl?"

The thought of his warm palm on my bare ass does strange things low in my belly. "I don't know what you're talking about." Moving a knight, I feign innocence.

"You know exactly what I'm talking about." He follows my lead, and his knight jumps over one of his pawns. "You're getting mouthy with me because you're upset over the distance I've put between us."

"How intuitive of you." I slide out another pawn.

"You feel rejected."

"That's not true."

It really is true, and I hate myself for the weakness. I didn't expect to feel this way, but I do, and it's causing chaos in my head. We advance several more pawns, losing casualties along the way, and then I move my queen, paying no attention to strategy.

When it comes to him I have no strategy.

His castle takes my queen.

He settles back in his seat, chin resting on his fist. "Take your time."

Letting out a sigh of frustration, I weigh my options. I could take his queen in two moves, but he'd only block it. The seconds tick past as I study the board, searching for a winning course of action I haven't yet found.

His patience is never-ending. He sits in that chair as if he owns it—because he does, and he owns me in this game. Just as I'm about to move my bishop, he breaks the silence.

"If you win, I'll make you come."

His promise tingles through my limbs, stirring excitement in my veins and flooding hot liquid to the apex of my thighs. I raise my gaze to his, taken aback by the desire in those sexy brown eyes.

"Are you trying to distract me?"

He shrugs. "Just providing incentive."

The promise of his hands on me is motivation enough... if I thought I could win.

But I won't, and he knows it.

"You tease me, Chancellor."

His mouth twitches at the purposeful slip-up. "I've got you in two moves."

"How can you be so sure?"

"I know how to play the game, Novalee."

He sure does. He brought me in here to dangle the forbidden fruit in front of me, only to yank it out of reach. Instead of moving a bishop, I send my knight jumping two squares forward and one to the right, and just as he promised, he puts me in check. There's only one spot for my king to go.

And after I take my turn it's game over, because he has me cornered.

"Is this your idea of punishment?" I move my king into inevitable surrender. "Watching me lose?"

"I haven't gotten to your punishment yet." Liam slides his queen into position. "Mate." His eyes tangle with mine, rife with heat. I fail to breathe, overcome by the seducing quiet between us.

"You won," I say with a hard swallow.

"I did." He rises, blatant longing playing on his face, and holds out a hand.

I slide my palm along his, my body tingling from anticipation. I'm nervous and scared all at once. He's not as put-together today, with his hair in slight disarray and cufflinks removed, sleeves pushed to the elbow. He leads me up the three short steps to the bed and orders me to bend over the end. As I drape the comforter, I'm acutely aware that this is where he sleeps.

Alone.

Probably naked.

Does he pleasure himself between these sheets?

Does he think of me when he does?

"Spread your legs."

Heartbeat doing double time, I part my thighs. He lifts the back of my skirt, and I hear him suck in a breath.

Because I'm not wearing panties.

"Jesus, Novalee."

I want him to touch me. Badly. Obsessively. It's all I've thought about for the last sixteen days while he shut himself away from me.

Protecting us both, he claims.

"Please," I whisper, arching my spine.

He splays his hand where my ass cheeks meet, the tips of his fingers dipping close to where I want them.

So close.

But he doesn't move. His hot and heavy palm lingers on my bottom, just a tease. A promise. My heartbeat thunders in my ears, booming one…two…three times.

Then he smacks my ass.

There's no yelp or cry of pain. Only a whimper of need as his palm connects with my flesh again, softly and with purpose, those fingers teasingly close to the spot that aches for him.

I'm on fire, turning to ash for this man.

"Please," I say again as my limbs shake.

"What are you begging for?"

Everything.

I can't verbalize what I want, unable to form the words. Because they're a foreign plea on my tongue.

I want to come.

He smacks me again, fingers grazing the wetness between my legs.

He knows what I want, and he's toying with me.

I *need* to come.

It's rising inside me, as forceful as a tsunami. As tremendous as the sea itself.

"Is this what you want, my sweet girl?" His fingers plunge, sliding through my arousal, and he holds them there as I writhe.

"More," I groan.

His thumb pushes against my anus, adding enough pressure to make me go still. He's cupping me, refusing to give me more. His torso blankets my back, and he yanks my head up by the hair.

"How quickly you forget. You lost the game."

"Please," I whine, unable to take in a full breath.

Not with the way my heart gallops.

Not so long as his fingers press against my clit, unmoving. A relentless taunt.

I choke out his name, and he shudders, breath hot and raspy on my neck.

"You don't know the level of control I'm clinging to right now." Slowly, his thumb invades my backside, burning...burning...

I whimper again, this time from pain.

"You're sexier than any woman I've been with. Fully innocent and too damn responsive. I know what the glove of your mouth feels like, Novalee." His thumb gains another inch, and I cry out in agony. "My cock is dying to know what this feels like too."

"Stop!"

Immediately, he pulls away. For several moments, I brace against the bed, chest heaving, terrified by what he implied as his thumb violated my ass. Footsteps thud across the room. A chair scrapes the floor. I push off the mattress and face him.

"Some of my brothers *won't* stop." Darkness shrouds his gaze, accompanied by a crease of anger between his brows. "They'll use your ass, and there isn't a thing I can do to stop them, Novalee."

His statement shakes me to the core, spoken with harsh truth and a hint of helpless frustration, and I almost crumble. "I don't want to leave you."

Abandoning his chair and the distance between us, he frames my face in his warm hands. "But you must. Our time together is dwindling fast. I *need* you to behave yourself. Heath won't tolerate your attitude."

"I'll try."

"You'll do more than try." His voice thickens, deep with a warning. "Because the next time you speak to me with such disrespect, I won't leave you with a throbbing pussy—I'll leave welts on your ass. Is that clear?"

Tears sting my eyes, and I blink them back. "Y-yes."

"You may return to your quarters. You're to stay there until dinner."

8

Liam's threat plays in my head on a nerve-wracking loop. His harsh words struck me in the heart, bringing about an inescapable melancholy that's only exacerbated by the rain. I try to escape my impending reality by visiting the boutiques on the main part of the island with my ladies.

The thing about reality? It's rarely avoidable.

So is the rain attacking in a torrential downpour. The relentless precipitation has been a steady annoyance for days. We return to the tower drenched and all shopped-out. The bodyguard Liam insisted on—a stoic man with muscled arms and a thick neck—opens the door of the main entrance, and my ladies and I spill inside, dripping rainwater everywhere.

"Today wasn't the best day for an outing," Faye says, letting the bags she's holding drop to her feet.

"It's as good a day as any." Elise sets the rest of our haul on the floor. "Jerome says it rains at least 250 days out of the year here."

Jerome is the wealthy businessman who's been courting Elise for the last few weeks.

Faye rolls her eyes. "Jerome this and Jerome that."

Elise shoots her a rare scowl. "You don't have to be catty about it."

"Sorry," Faye says, sheepish. "I'll try to rein it in."

Selma appears from the kitchen. "The chancellor would like to see you in the library," she tells me as she hands out towels to the three of us.

"Do you know why he requested to see me?"

"It's not a request. I don't know his reasons."

I dry my hair, patting down the combination of strands and braids, and a tingle of wary excitement rushes through me. Ever since our chess game, things have become more strained, teeming with undeniable sexual tension. He hasn't sought me out at all.

Until now.

I part ways with my ladies and take the journey down the long hallway. My dress sticks to my skin from the rain, but I forgo a trip to the penthouse to change first, much too eager to see Liam. As I pass the portraits of the Brotherhood's ancestors, the portrayal of Evangeline Castle draws my focus. What must it have been like to be in her position, locked away and used by twelve men? Did she grow to love any of them?

One?

Two?

Three or more?

I can't fathom falling in love with two men, but I can't deny I'm attracted to both Liam and Sebastian.

The latter makes zero sense.

I turn down another hallway, and that's when I realize I took a wrong turn. As if my thoughts conjured his presence, Sebastian's raspy timbre filters into the hall from an ajar door on the left.

"Fucking gorgeous, Mona."

A feminine voice murmurs something in response, words indiscernible, and I slow my steps, drawn to what lies beyond that door. Every bone in my body bids me to keep going, to not look into that room and lay eyes on him. To not give him another opportunity to unleash his cruelty on me.

Apparently, I'm a glutton for punishment. Holding my breath, I peek around the edge of the doorframe, and the depraved sight before my eyes knocks the air from my lungs. Breath escapes me in a silent whoosh.

A woman is spread out on a lounge, her deep burgundy locks flowing over creamy, bare breasts. It's the pose that has me in a trance. Her legs are bent, splayed in repose, the shaven lips of her womanhood on proud display. She's without shame or modesty, and something about her confidence calls to me.

Sebastian has his back to me as he transfers the likeness of her onto his canvas, and I can't help but study the broadness of his shoulders, or the way his dark blond hair sticks up in dishevelment.

He's the polar opposite of Liam.

Brazen where the chancellor is reserved.

Carefree instead of controlled.

Unrestrained sexy compared to Liam's more classic dark looks.

Sebastian's low-slung jeans steal my attention as his

brush hits the canvas with confident strokes. The man paints as well as he fills out a pair of jeans.

"Bash," the woman says, and when I turn my attention back to her, I find her deep brown eyes on me. She points in my direction, and Sebastian turns around before I can duck into the hall.

The instant his blue eyes meet mine, I'm frozen, caught red-handed, cheeks hot with embarrassment. A lifetime seems to pass in the lock of our gazes. My pulse speeds up. His brows narrow. I run the tip of my tongue along the seam of my mouth, and when his attention stalls on my lips, I can't help but tuck the bottom one between my teeth.

He frowns, sets down the paintbrush, and that's when I spring into motion, darting down the hall as fast as my jittery legs will carry me.

But footsteps chase me, accompanied by deep and harsh breaths. A large, warm hand clamps around my bicep and yanks me to a stop. I turn slowly, every tortuous beat of my heart sounding-off in my ears as I face the accusation in his brilliant stare.

"Did you get a good eyeful?"

"I-I didn't mean—"

"Didn't mean to spy on me?" he cuts in, invading my personal space. He's not as tall as Liam, but his presence is overbearing enough. As I try to retreat, his fingers dig into my arm, making escape impossible.

"I wasn't spying."

"Does Liam know you're down here?"

"Yes." Though I'm sure the chancellor wouldn't be happy to find us in our current position—his hand gripping my bicep as my bosom heaves against his chest.

The furrow between Sebastian's brows deepens. "I'm surprised he let his little pet roam free."

"He requested my presence in the library."

"This wing is off-limits to you. It's reserved for my public studio."

"I'm sorry. I didn't know."

"Well now you know."

"It won't happen again."

"Make sure it doesn't." He lets go of my arm, and I miss the warmth of his touch, which is crazy because he's treated me with nothing but disdain every time we've crossed paths.

But I can't deny I'm alive from the intensity in his gaze, the seriousness of his brow, the way he's clenching those large hands. I imagine them gripping my thighs and flush even hotter.

What is wrong with me?

It's not like me to become so tongue-tied in the company of a man.

But maybe that's the problem—Sebastian isn't some average guy standing in front of me. He's one-hundred percent alpha with a legal and binding claim on my life.

He's the kind of man who paints naked women for fun.

And in four months, he'll have total dominion over my body.

A shudder tears through me, laden with arousal at the unwelcome thought. As if he senses my reaction to his nearness, he steps forward again, crowding my personal space. Inch by inch, he pushes me against the wall. My spine bumps against cold stone, and I gasp as something hard presses into my thigh.

Sebastian is sporting an erection, and though he was just painting an attractive nude woman not five minutes ago, I'm positive his hard-on is for me.

"You might as well make yourself useful since you interrupted my session," he says, voice a sexy murmur as he sifts my blond locks through his fingers.

"What do you mean?"

"Provide me with a little inspiration." His body is hard against mine, tempting my soft curves to mold to the contour of his muscles, the planes of his abs.

I stare at his lips. "I'm not taking my clothes off for you."

"You could wear your hair instead. It's amazing."

The compliment is unexpected, and I stutter out a thank-you.

"I've wanted to paint you from the moment I first saw you."

I blink, and in that millimeter of a second, I imagine myself sprawled in front of him like the woman he left in the other room. No clothing, legs open to his gaze as he captures how he sees me on canvas with bold, sure strokes.

No exam bench or hostility.

No other men.

But would he see me as a girl or a woman? Something tells me he'd see me as the latter.

"You're thinking about it, aren't you? Would you spread your legs and let me paint your cunt, princess?" His eyes are alight with amused curiosity, but the vulgarity of his words spark the opposite in me.

"Let me go," I demand, pushing against his chest.

The amusement fades from his expression, and he separates himself from me in the space of a second.

As if I burned him.

"Forgive me," he says. "For a moment there, I thought your fully formed tits meant you'd grown out of the child queen I met six years ago."

Indignation takes hold of me. The last thing I want is for him to see me as a child. "I'm eighteen now."

"Like I said. A *child*."

I resist the urge to stomp my feet and argue with him, as I'm sure that sort of behavior will only prove his point. "You're insufferable. Why do you have to be such a jerk?"

With a sigh, he takes another step away from me. "It's in my DNA, princess. You're too innocent to see it for what it is."

"I'll kindly remind you I'm a queen."

His lips twitch with renewed amusement. "No reminder needed. I've got plenty of pressure from my family to ensure a marriage to you."

"You don't sound happy about it."

"I've accepted it."

"Am I not what you expected?"

His gaze travels the length of my body, heating me all over again. "No, my *queen*. I expected a prim and proper child less appealing than a nun. What you are is innocence wrapped in the body of a porn star."

I grit my teeth. Rising to his bait will only heighten the tension between us because Sebastian is fire and passion rolled into one impossibly gorgeous, unstable male. Movement catches my attention, and a glance over his shoulder reveals his gorgeous subject standing in the doorway of his studio, her body wrapped in a black satin sheet.

"Are you coming back, Sebastian?"

The very essence of her is sinful, and I've never envied another woman until now. Her attention shifts, and when I follow the direction of her gaze, I find Liam standing in the shadows of the hall, arms crossed and mouth grim with displeasure.

9

Dinner is unbearable. Tense and silent—only the scrape of flatware on china breaks the disquiet. He said he's not upset with me. Sebastian's the target of his anger.

But deep down, I don't believe him.

"Why did you want to see me in the library today?"

For the first time since we sat down at the table, his eyes flick up to meet mine. "Heath needs to fit you for your crown."

I blink. "What crown?"

"It's Heath's gift to you. There will be a coronation after the auction."

His words are a stark, painful reminder that my days with him are numbered.

"I rescheduled the meeting. He's coming to the penthouse tomorrow." He gives me a pointed look. "You need to be on your best behavior."

"Okay." I go back to pushing manicotti around my plate.

The ensuing seconds eat away at my composure, and I

tap my heel against the floor. The food is flavorless as it slides down my throat.

"I can't stand the thought of them touching you."

Startled by his confession, I raise my gaze to his. "I can't stand it either."

With the exception of one.

The tick in Liam's jaw tells me he knows it too.

"You're attracted to him." Not a question, but a fact that sketches jealousy across his face.

"I'd rather be here with you than with anyone else."

"You only say that because my brothers are unknown territory to you. You're scared of the unknown."

That's probably true, but there's no denying my attraction to Liam, or the connection I feel to him. It's been there from the beginning.

More silence stews between us.

Heavy with the things we've said.

And the things we don't.

"Tomorrow's my birthday." His announcement fractures the spiraling tension, offering a welcome change of subject.

"How old will you be?"

"Twenty-four."

"Do you have plans to celebrate?"

"All of them involve you and the many things we shouldn't do."

"Why shouldn't we?" I ask, barely breathing.

"I'm not a patient man, Novalee. You'll leave my house in a few days, and I won't be allowed to touch you for the next eleven months."

"But you're the chancellor."

"Yes, my word holds the most authority on policy and

business decisions, but the Brotherhood's contract regarding you is outside the scope of that. My only advantage is having you first."

I gnaw on my lip, afraid to voice my next question. "What happens if you do...touch me...when I'm under someone else's authority?"

"Touching you without permission?" He rakes his fingers through his hair. "Corporal punishment, at the least..."

"And at most?"

"My right to bid in the auction could be revoked."

My mind flashes to yesterday when Sebastian had me against the wall. "Is that why you're furious with Sebastian? Because he touched me?"

"He crossed a line, but he didn't engage in a sexual act with you." He pauses a beat, fingers tapping his annoyance on the table. "That's me showing my penchant for jealousy."

I like that he's jealous. It's a shameful thing to admit, even to myself. "What constitutes a sexual act?"

"Jesus," he mutters, letting out a breath. "Touching your breasts or other intimate areas, kissing, using you for pleasure..." He raises his eyes to the ceiling as if praying for fortitude. "Straight up sex."

"Liam." The softness of his name on my lips brings his focus back to me, and I feel my face redden with heat. "I want those things with you." It's a brazen confession—one I can't believe I put into words.

"If I touch you...*really* fucking touch you...I don't know how I'll keep my hands to myself until the auction."

Dinner is forgotten between us on the table, cold and tasteless. The only thing I want to taste is him. I pull up the memory of his cock in my mouth, and the resulting ache is so intense that I squeeze my thighs together.

"What's going through your head?" he asks as if he senses the direction of my thoughts.

"That first day in the library, when I was on my knees..." I pause, hesitant to continue. "I was thinking of how I've wanted to do it again."

Muttering a curse, he stands. "You can't help but tempt me." He picks up our plates and heads toward the kitchen where Selma waits, out of earshot to give us privacy. "I have some work to finish before bed. You should get some sleep too."

That's the last I see of him all evening. I take a bath with the latest fantasy novel I'm caught up in, but not even reading about dragons and curses distracts my mind from Liam Castle.

I'm tempted to slide my hand between my legs to find relief, but I don't.

Because he forbade it.

And I want that first with him.

I want him to take it so the others can't.

I want him to win the auction, too, so the others have no chance of stealing my virginity.

Sleep doesn't come easy. I toss and turn for hours, wracked by images of twelve sets of hands touching me, punishing me, using me for their pleasure.

The reality is terrifying, the pictures in my head irrevocable. I'm certain I'll be up all night plagued by duty and destiny...

Until the bed shifts, and I realize I dozed off. At first, I think I'm caught between that weird moment between deep sleep and the more restless, partially alert variety. The kind of slumber where you twitch and it feels like someone's sitting on the bed. It's an eerie sensation, feeling a phantom weight when you know you're alone.

Except...I'm *not* alone.

With a gasp, I lurch upright, and a firm hand sends me sprawling to the mattress again.

"Do you know what time it is?" Liam's voice hovers only inches away in the darkness, his tone infused with the lustful rasp I crave.

I swallow hard, caught off-guard. "The middle of the night?"

"It's past midnight."

His speech is off, slower than usual and lacking inhibition. If I couldn't tell by his mannerisms, the spiciness of whiskey in the air is telling enough.

"Are you drunk?"

"I never drink to excess. I'm merely armed with the right amount of celebratory scotch."

"What are you celebrating?"

"My birthday."

My gaze darts to the nightstand and the green glow of the numbers on the clock sitting there. It's past midnight, indeed.

I make out the outline of his face in my darkened quarters. "Happy Birthday, Chancellor."

The bed shifts again as he sits on his haunches, and then his hands are on my chest, knuckles skimming my ribs as he tears my pajama shirt from breast to navel. Buttons go flying. He lifts me long enough to remove the ruined top, and my nipples peak as if expecting the heat of his gaze.

The warmth of his mouth.

The pinch of his fingers.

His hands drift over the sensitive buds, and I can't help but arch into his warm palms.

"Have you touched yourself without my permission, Novalee?"

I shake my head, moaning something close to a "no," my body begging for more. Begging for what he's refused to give me.

"If I make you come, I want something from you in return. Consider it a birthday request."

"Anything."

"For the next eleven months after you leave my house, I want your word that you won't touch yourself when you're alone."

"What if I'm ordered to touch myself?"

"That's out of your control. But what you do when you're alone..." He braces himself above me and dips his head, mouth grazing my ear. "That's up to you, and I want you to promise me your fingers won't come in contact with your beautiful pussy."

"You'll make me come?"

"All night long, my sweet girl."

I shudder in the circle of his arms. "What if I'm thinking of you when I touch myself?"

"Those are fighting words." He groans, and then his mouth covers mine, the weight of his body pressing us into the mattress as he plunders my mouth. I thrust my fingers into his thick hair, pulling at the strands as I wrap my legs around his waist. The position brings us together in an explosive way, his hardness against my softness.

Tearing away with a painful groan, he crawls to the end of the bed and grabs my ankles. Next thing I know, I'm sliding down the mattress. He hefts me over his shoulder and carries me from my quarters to his. The door barely makes a sound as it shuts us away, alone, in the one place I'm not allowed.

The place where he sleeps.

The place he swore he wouldn't have me until after we're married.

He pushes his pajama pants down his legs and kicks the clothing free. I freeze, ogling his glorious naked body. Guided by moonlight, I take him in from the definition of his biceps to the muscular build of his thighs.

And everything in between.

Breaths shallow and thready, I dart my tongue out to wet my lips. His nostrils flare, and a low growl emanates from his throat. He's at his most base self, raw and animalistic and struggling to hold himself in check.

"If it weren't for the contract," he says, fisting his hands at his sides, "I'd make you bleed for me. Only me, Novalee."

But there *is* a contract, and we're both bound by it.

He takes a step closer, eating up the inches between us, and the spiciness of his cologne infuses my nose. His rough breathing fills my ears. I crane my neck to meet his eyes.

"I'm yours...however you want me."

"I want you naked."

He issues the demand with soft-spoken patience, but I sense the urgency in him as I remove the last of my clothing. It's the same desperate need rushing through my veins, heating my blood to boiling. As soon as we're both without clothing or shame—without reservation or doubt—I drop to my knees and put my mouth on him. I don't think about it. Don't question it.

All I know is I've longed to taste him again.

His fingers stab through my hair, and instead of pulling me closer, he yanks me back. "Not yet."

"Why not?"

"I want to watch you come first." He pulls me into his arms and carries me up the platform to his bed. "Do you trust me?"

My answer is immediate. "Yes."

He sets me on the edge, and I brace my hands behind me, my focus glued to his every move. Standing between my thighs, he wraps his hand around his cock. The vision of him, cast in silhouette from the night, conjures the likeness of Adonis, the god of beauty and desire.

Because he's full of both and the keeper of seduction as he rubs the head of his shaft between my folds, spreading my wetness.

His trophy.

"Liam," I groan as my strength flees, leaving me trembling and unable to prop myself on my arms. I fall to the mattress and clutch the bedding. My skin flushes hot.

Too hot.

I'm about to combust.

"What are you doing to me?"

"I'm keeping your body pure. Your head and heart are another matter."

With one hand, he braces above me and angles his mouth over mine. The glorious friction between us intensifies. Sweat and lust drench my skin, and I can barely form a thought. All I can do is moan his name against his lips, over and over again as the head of his cock rubs me to madness.

"Liam!" Back bowing, I fist the blanket, and my upper body rises off the mattress. Everything below the waist is owned by him.

"That's it," he groans. "Come on my cock. Come on it hard, my sweet girl."

He doesn't stop the friction until the last intense wave releases me. I'm floating on some ethereal cloud of completion when he pulls me up by my noodle-like arms.

"Down," he says with a nod to the floor.

Too wrecked to stay on my feet anyway, I slide to the floor, knees buckling, and he pushes into my waiting mouth. The combined taste of us is a taboo treat on my tongue. I'm delirious as he thrusts his way to release, smashing the back of my head into the side of the mattress. I splay my hands on his thighs, nails biting into his skin.

Because I'm trapped, sandwiched between the mattress and the furious need driving his cock into my throat.

"Damn," he chokes out, followed by another string of expletives that launch from his lips. A shudder seizes his muscles, thighs going tense under my hands.

Then he surrenders, his grasp on my hair a painful burn as he shoots his seed down my throat.

And I never thought I'd witness the day when Liam Castle would cry out my name.

10

Naked bodies. Satin sheets. A decadent sense of satisfaction when I open my eyes and find his gaze on me. I stretch, sliding my leg between his. "What time is it?"

"Almost lunchtime."

I'm not surprised since we were up until the wee hours of the morning discovering each other. I now know that nibbling on his earlobe makes him hard. Running a hand down his abs to his belly button makes his breath stutter. Dragging a finger along the length of his cock makes it twitch.

Putting it in my mouth makes him lose his mind.

I made him lose his mind more than once.

He discovered things about me, too. Things I didn't know about. Like when he traced my areola, and it tickled instead of aroused. Or how anticipation shook my bones when he trailed his tongue up my inner thigh. How soft and silky his hair was in my fingers as I clutched him between my legs.

How I pulsed on his tongue for what seemed like forever.

It was a magical night—one I wish had never ended—because the faint ticking of his watch is a constant reminder that time doesn't slow down for anything.

Rolling me to my back, Liam presses me into the mattress. "How am I going to let you go?"

"Don't let me go."

"You know I don't have a choice."

"Will I see you...after I leave?" My finger traces a path over the curve of his shoulder.

"I'll make sure you do." A shadow darkens his features. "But we'll have to keep our hands to ourselves. We definitely can't do this." He presses his warm lips to mine, tongue seeking entrance, and I sigh into his kiss.

How will I make it eleven months? It seems like an eternity.

Liam breaks the kiss, and I ask the question that hurts my heart the most. "What if you don't win?" I can't bring myself to think of the possible outcomes. All twelve of them.

How can it be anyone *but* him?

"I don't want you to worry about that now." He holds me by the chin. "A lot can happen between now and then. You could fall in love with someone who isn't me."

A contemptuous blue gaze invades my mind, unwelcome and unwanted.

"You're the one I want."

"I'm the one you're comfortable with. You haven't had the chance to get to know my brothers."

I narrow my eyes. "Are you having second thoughts about winning the auction?"

"No." His thumb plays on my lower lip. "But if I'm not who you want by the time the auction arrives, then I won't compete to win."

"Am I not worth fighting for?"

"You are, my sweet girl." He pulls away and sits at the edge of the bed. "But your happiness is worth more to me than winning."

I sit up, tugging the sheet to the top of my breasts, suddenly unsure and shy. He didn't take my virginity last night, but he might as well have. He stole a piece of my soul I'll never get back. "I want it to be you, Liam."

"If you still feel that way eleven months from now, I'll do everything in my power to ensure it's me." He stands and takes a step forward, keeping his back to me. "I need to shower and dress. You should do the same. Heath will be here in an hour."

He disappears into the bathroom and shuts the door, and it's like a wall coming down between us all over again.

11

Dressed in a black chiffon skirt and a sleeveless top, I perch on the lounge in the main sitting room. By all appearances, I'm prepared to face the day, makeup flawless and hair silky smooth. Anyone sending a cursory glance my way would think I was ready for this meeting with the man who will reign over me in the coming weeks.

But I'm not.

"Stop your fidgeting, my sweet girl." Liam gently scolds me from his chair.

Only then do I realize the rhythmic bounce of my foot, one crossed over the other. I cease the nervous movement just as Selma appears in the archway.

"Chancellor, Mr. Bordeaux is here to see you."

Liam nods. "Send him in."

She steps out of view, and the man I remember from the dinner and medical exam takes her place. He's taller than Sebastian, but a few inches shy of Liam's six-foot frame. His expensive black suit, meticulously pressed, doesn't have a wrinkle in sight. There's an undeniable seriousness about him...and a coldness that makes me shiver.

His hazel eyes zero in on me. "My queen."

I dip my head. "I'm unsure of how I should address you."

"Mr. Bordeaux will do." He waltzes into the sitting room and settles next to me on the lounge.

Liam hasn't moved an inch. He's as stoic as the man next to me.

"I assume the chancellor informed you of the reason behind this visit?"

"Yes."

"Yes, *Mr. Bordeaux*," he corrects, mouth sloping into a frown. "And I expect you on your knees when you greet me in the future." He shoots Liam an irritated glance. "In fact, she should be in that position now."

His words raise my hackles, and before I attempt to form a response, Liam cuts in.

"You don't have that kind of authority in this house."

"Soon enough, my queen." Heath removes a ribbon of measuring tape from his pocket. "I need to take your measurements." He gestures to the top of my head, and I remain still as he wraps the tape around my skull.

But I'm quaking on the inside and trying to hold it together. In a few days, Liam won't be around to protect me from this man.

"Does my queen have any design requests?" he asks as he marks the measurements in a black portfolio.

"Your queen does not." I can't help it—the snarky edge sneaks into my tone before I can stop it, and I sense Liam's sigh rather than hear it. The displeased pull of Heath's dark brows sends dread through me, and I rush to temper my tone. "But thank you for giving me the option."

He shuts the portfolio with a decisive *snap*. "Chancellor, I believe you've been lax in handling Miss Van Buren."

Liam hasn't moved from his position. Sitting to my right, chin in hand, he watches with hooded eyes that hide any hint of what he's thinking. "I've handled her just fine."

"Her attitude is unacceptable."

"We have differing views on what's acceptable."

Heath stands with a scowl. "She needs a training session in the dungeon."

"That won't happen while she's in my house."

Heath swivels his attention between the chancellor and me, jaw rigid and cold, hazel eyes squinting with frustration. "That will be the first thing she receives when she comes to mine." He strides out of the sitting room, and when the front door of the penthouse slams upon his exit, I startle.

Liam rises. "I can't let your behavior slide."

I bow my head in shame because he warned me. "I'm sorry."

"Apologies won't save you from the dungeon, and they won't spare you now." The sound of a belt buckle lifts my gaze. I'm stricken as I watch him slide the thick leather strap from his pant loops.

"Liam, please."

"Take off your skirt."

Blinking back tears, I stand and slide the waistband down my thighs. The light material pools around my feet and I step out of the puddle of chiffon.

"Climb up," he says, waving at the chair he just vacated.

He loops the belt in his fist. "You can hold on to the back for support."

"*Please*," I beg again as the tears spill.

"Do as I say!"

His thundering baritone destroys the last of my composure, and I bawl as I climb onto the chair. It's not the threat of pain that bothers me the most.

It's the betrayal storming through me, devastating my heart in its violent path.

I embrace the cushioned back as his steps carry him closer. Those purposeful footfalls stall behind me, and he sucks in a deep breath. I wait, muscles quivering as gooseflesh crawls down my naked backside.

He promised welts if I misbehaved again.

He said it's a matter of consistency, so I know the first strike is coming.

He's a man of his word.

More seconds slip by, and I hold my breath as the salt of his betrayal drips down my cheeks.

Still...the first strike doesn't come.

"Goddamnit, Novalee." Something thumps to the floor.

I'm frozen in my vulnerable position, scared to believe he changed his mind.

"Get down." His voice is soft, defeated.

A sob of relief escapes me. I turn to face him on shaky limbs, cheeks bathed in tears as I wrap my arms around myself. "You couldn't do it."

"No." He takes me by the chin. "The thought of hurting you sickens me." His grip tightens, incongruent with his words. "Heath doesn't suffer from the same affliction. His rules are rigid, Novalee. He'll hurt you when you break them."

"Why?" The question is little more than a hoarse whisper. I clear my throat. "Why would he want to hurt me?"

"It's just who he is." He lets go of me and takes a step back, putting three feet of space between us. "And he won't budge. Once he's set his mind on something, there's no undoing it." His regretful gaze darts in the direction of the chair at my back. "He won't change his mind about the dungeon."

"I don't want to go."

"You have to." He's shaking, composure in tatters as he drags a hand through his hair. "And once you do, I can't protect you."

TAURUS

BOOK TWO

1

APRIL 21ST

5,760 minutes. 96 hours. Four days. Roughly, that's how long it's been since Heath Bordeaux fit me for my crown. Those days snuck by in the blink of an eye, in the microseconds a bolt of lightning steals when striking the ground...in the time it takes to break a heart.

Leaving the haven of Liam Castle broke mine.

"He should be here with you," Faye says as we approach the library on the first floor of the tower. Elise nods in agreement.

"He decided against it," I say, doing my best not to chew my nails.

The chancellor's absence is like a gushing wound in my chest. I'm devastated he chose not to escort me himself—leaving my ladies to do it—but I understand why he made the decision.

I think back to my last ten minutes with him, on the cusp of his penthouse door.

"I'm not ready to say goodbye," I'd pleaded, tears stinging my eyes as his hands rose to frame my face. His thumbs had brushed along my cheekbones as if preparing to wipe the pain away between us.

"This isn't goodbye, my sweet girl."

"It feels a lot like goodbye, Chancellor."

A melancholy smile quirked at the corners of his lips. "I know we've grown close enough this past month for you to be comfortable using my name."

"The title just slipped out," I'd lied, hoping he'd scold me, spank me, lock me up and keep me as punishment for my refusal to use his name. Anything but sending me out that door.

He'd raised a brow upon my feigned innocence. "If you're begging for my hand as a delaying tactic, it won't work. I won't cause your tardiness for the inevitable."

By the inevitable he meant the start of my prison sentence with Heath Bordeaux.

I couldn't have argued with him even if I'd wanted to, because in the next instant he'd kissed me. It hadn't tasted like goodbye. In the sweep of our tongues, I'd found quiet desperation. Sweet sorrow. A promise for so much more, whether it be eleven days or eleven months down the line.

"Go," he'd rasped against my damp lips, forehead pressed to mine. His hand landed on the door handle, threatening to thrust me into the supervision of my ladies who waited on the other side of the barrier locking us in this private moment.

"Don't make me go."

The handle turned—an almost indiscernible click. "You have to. Don't make this harder than it already is, Novalee." His warm breath on my cheek, followed by the press of his lips, would have to sustain me until I saw him again.

I cling to the memory now as his maid stops in front of the massive doors of the library. "Are you ready?" Selma asks, and I think I spot a sorrowful hint in the pinch of her coral lips. She's in full uniform, a no-nonsense bun holding her graying blond hair at the nape.

"Yes, I'm...ready."

It's a lie. I'm as ready for Heath Bordeaux as I was the day he fit me for my crown and revealed a taste of his unforgiving, obstinate nature.

Selma knocks three times. A deep male voice calls for us to come in, and Selma allows us entry into the room where it all began. It's a light and airy space, despite the masculine bookcases that surround the comfortable seating arrangements inviting meetings among leaders.

And the passing-around of queens.

Heath Bordeaux is waiting by the south-facing windows. His back is to me, but I recognize him by his rigid stature. His black hair sheens silvery in the late morning rays pouring through the arched glass in front of him. A blond man I've never seen before stands at attention near him, his posture as rigid as the man who will have dominion over me for the next month.

Mr. Bordeaux turns, and those hazel eyes shoot ice through me. They're beautiful eyes set in a traditionally handsome face, but something about him is...

Cold.

Vacant.

To make matters worse, he's glaring at me.

"Your ladies may return to their quarters. You won't need their services while you're a guest in my house."

His statement hits me like a sneak attack—a wave that

rises from nowhere and knocks me down—and I drop to my knees.

"Please, Mr. Bordeaux. Don't send my ladies away. I beg of you."

They're all I have in this place. The only two people keeping me sane.

"That isn't for you to decide." He nods toward his silent companion, who steps forward upon command. "My manservant will escort your ladies back to where they belong."

Faye takes a brave step toward Mr. Bordeaux. "This isn't right. I'm not—"

Cutting her off, I jump to my feet and hug her tight enough to silence her objection. Elise dabs at her eyes in my peripheral. "Shh, it's okay," I tell her in a whisper. "Go, *please*."

Mr. Bordeaux is *not* Liam, with his gentle authority and quiet leniency. I don't know who the man from the House of Taurus is, but he's not someone you disobey or argue with, and it would wreck me to watch him punish Faye because of her loyalty to me.

"He can't keep us away from you for a whole month."

I pull back and meet her sable eyes. "Yes, he can, Faye."

With the exception of taking my virginity, he can do whatever he wants.

"But you're my queen." Faye blinks rapidly, and it's enough to harden my heart against the man forcing us apart because she doesn't get emotional. She gets angry, indignant, righteous.

She doesn't do tears, but she's holding them back now.

"As your queen, I'm ordering you to go. I'll be okay. I promise."

"Faye," Elise says in a soft lilt, "we have to do what's best for Novalee." She grabs Faye's hand, giving it a subtle tug, and wordlessly, they follow Mr. Bordeaux's manservant out of the library.

I'm frozen to the spot, fighting tears, fearful of turning around and confronting the heartless man who just sent my only support system away for the next month.

"Don't stand with your back to me."

I pivot. "Why did you send them away?" Anger vibrates in my limbs, rushing through my blood until I'm brimming with it. I embrace the sting in my eyes, unwilling to shed a single tear in his presence.

He appears unmoved by my outburst, his expression wooden as his stride brings him within arm's reach. "It's not your place to question me." He points to the floor. "Kneel."

I go down, my mind flashing back to a month ago when my uncle forced me to my knees for the chancellor. Unwittingly, my attention darts to Mr. Bordeaux's zipper.

Unlike Liam, he's not aroused.

I cling to that small favor.

"Down on your haunches."

My ass meets the back of my heels.

"Bow your head."

Aiming my gaze at the floor, I follow his movement from the corner of my eye as he wanders behind me.

"Hands on your thighs, palms up." He murmurs his approval after I do what I'm told. "Good. This is how you'll kneel in my presence. Is that clear?"

"Yes, Mr. Bordeaux," I say, lifting my head enough to peek at him as he approaches the other side of me.

"I see you've learned a little respect since our meeting in the chancellor's penthouse." Three more steps brings him full circle. "But there's room for improvement."

My pulse ratchets as one word blares in my mind, as loud and panic inducing as a scream.

Dungeon.

"I'll do my best to learn, Mr. Bordeaux."

Anything to get through the next thirty days unscathed.

"Queens are to be seen, not heard. You will not speak unless spoken to. Do you understand?"

I don't understand at all.

"Do you understand, my queen?" he enunciates slowly.

I stutter out an answer. "Y-yes...but...what if I need to say something?"

"It's yes, *Mr. Bordeaux.*" His ire lands in the thump of his shoes as he circles me once more. "If you feel the need to speak, then you'll raise your hand, and I'll either grant permission or deny it."

I lick my lips, eliminating the question weighing on my tongue.

The one I can't ask.

The one I'm afraid to learn the answer to.

What happens if I break his rules?

"We'll begin with a training session in the dungeon. You need to know this isn't a punishment. I'm giving you the necessary information and training so you know, without a doubt, what your duties and boundaries are."

Maybe this won't be so bad. Maybe his cold detachment

will mean more distance between us. The lump of dread in my belly warns otherwise.

Mr. Bordeaux thrusts out a hand. "You may rise."

I get to my feet, and despite the alarm blaring through my head, I raise my eyes to his as our palms press together.

Displeasure pulls at his mouth. "We have a lot to cover." With a tug of my hand, he urges me toward the door, and I follow him as the hairs on the back of my neck stand on end.

2
———

I don't have many negative memories of my childhood before my parents' plane went down. The first twelve years of my life were filled with love, laughter, and a sense of security I'm not sure I'll ever experience again.

But one incident springs to the forefront of my mind as I descend a steep staircase behind Mr. Bordeaux, scones flooding warm light onto the brick walls as our feet scuttle down utilitarian plank steps.

It was the year before my parents died, and Faye and I escaped into the wine cellar, pretending to run from an evil dragon that would take us to the Black Prince—a handsome young boy who intended to enslave us in the tower of his castle.

Instead, we'd ended up enslaving ourselves in the cellar, trapped by an ill-fated jammed door and a busted light maintenance hadn't yet fixed since it went out the day before. To pass the hours until someone finally found us, we'd huddled in the dark, pretending the darkness kept us safe from the dragon.

But real life doesn't work like that. Darkness is a stifling entity I now despise, and there isn't a thing on Earth that will keep the dragon away.

My heart rate doubles by the time we reach the bottom of the staircase. Mr. Bordeaux uses a key to unlock a black iron gate, and I follow him deeper into the dim, cold space. If I had to choose one word to describe this place, it would be...

Horrifying.

It has the feel of a dungeon, with bars sectioning off cells to imprison the punished, and shackles hanging from the ceiling. But the word *dungeon* doesn't quite fit either. There's a decadence to the strange furnishings—the various high-end benches outfitted in dark red leather, and the massive bed sitting off by itself in another sectioned-off space, the sheets an onyx satin and the duvet a vibrant crimson.

The color of passion.

The color of pain.

The bed sits atop a cage, ominous in undertone. Thick leather cuffs dangle from the wooden bedposts, the sight of which shoots a shiver down the slope of my neck. My gaze stalls on an iron rack on the wall reserved for riding crops, whips, and other items that are equally terrifying and unknown. Opposite of that rack stands a wooden X, shackles waiting for wrists and ankles.

Mr. Bordeaux stalls as I take in my surroundings. I'm stupefied, my thoughts spinning in a fog. He turns to face me, and his eyes narrow as he waves a perfect, soft-looking hand. "Take off your clothes."

A bone-deep chill rushes through me, causing me to

hesitate. I'm so off kilter that I don't notice another person in the room, and the noise registers a second too late.

The cadence of a single footfall behind me.

A light rustle.

The fierce snap of leather an instant before it strikes me on the ass, issuing a sting forceful enough to send my teeth into a grind.

"Do as Mr. Bordeaux commands." The voice at my back is deep, harsh, leaving no room for doubt that he'll hit me again if I don't submit.

With shaking hands I grab the hem of my shirt and lift it over my breasts. I'm fumbling with the clasp of my undergarment when Mr. Bordeaux orders me to move faster.

"I-I'm sorry. I'm trying."

Another snap of the whip, harder this time, and I push to my toes with a sharp cry.

"Your master didn't give you permission to speak."

Mr. Bordeaux shakes his head. "I'm not her master."

"Down here we do things my way, and that means you *are* her master." More footsteps sound as I struggle out of the rest of my clothing, letting it gather around my feet in a messy, abandoned pile of lost dignity. The man with the whip comes into view, and I meet a set of familiar gray eyes.

Pax, from the House of Libra, and from what I recall during the medical examination, the keeper of the dungeon. I want to cower under his scrutiny, or at the least, palm my breasts so he'll stop molesting them with his lascivious gaze. Instead, I remain frozen with my hands dangling at my sides.

"Kneel," Mr. Bordeaux says, drawing my attention back to him.

I follow his command and assume the pose he wants, on my haunches, head bowed, hands on my thighs, palms up.

"You're quick to obey, but I shouldn't have to issue the order. Unless I say otherwise, this is how I expect you to present yourself." Three purposeful strides eat up the distance between us. "You will not move until I say otherwise, is that understood?"

A beat passes, and Pax's whip sends a soft caress across my breasts, prompting me to stumble over my answer. "I... yes, Mr. Bordeaux."

"You will kneel in this spot, alone and in the dark, until it becomes as natural as breathing."

Icy fear storms through me, and I bite my lip to keep from pleading for mercy. The two men leave without another word, locks clanking into place upon their exit. A melancholy echo reverberates through the chamber. I count the ensuing seconds in the beats of my heart, senses heightened in the quiet. Gooseflesh erupts on my skin, unhindered by clothing, and I want to wrap my arms around myself, hands rubbing the chill from my flesh until I find a hint of warmth, but I don't dare move.

Until the lights shut off, plunging me into darkness. I jerk forward, barely catching myself from losing my balance, and a whimper catches in my throat. This is the kind of blackness nightmares are made of—suffocating and oppressive as the air seems to crawl over my chilled skin like phantom fingers. The moonless sky during the Witching Hour would offer more light.

I squeeze my eyes shut and count the skittering tempo of my heartbeat.

One, two, three, four, five, six...

Liam's seductive brown eyes flash through my mind, and I latch onto the memory of him as if it's my only lifeline.

Because right now it is.

Seven, eight, nine, ten, eleven...

He's my armor against the dragon, and I replay the warmth of his fingers on my skin, the sigh of his breath on my lips, the cadence of his resonant voice.

Twelve, thirteen, fourteen, fifteen...

His head thrown back, mouth a tight line as pleasure seizes his limbs.

Sixteen, seventeen, eighteen...

The gruff cry that plays on his lips when he comes.

I let out a breath, clinging to the comfort of the memory. But it doesn't last forever. At some point, I'm so cold that my teeth chatter, despite the way my knees ache and burn.

And that's how Mr. Bordeaux and his dungeon sidekick find me when they return sometime later—my body tense from holding the degrading pose for so long, jaw rigid with tension, skin pebbled from the cold. Heavy footsteps surround me as I open my eyes and blink, my vision adjusting to the headache-inducing light.

"Posture," Pax calls out an instant before his whip strikes the flesh on my back. Gasping in stunned pain, I straighten my spine, teeth clenched tight.

"That's better. Slouching is never allowed."

"Neither is eye contact," Mr. Bordeaux says as he bends and lifts my chin. Unwittingly, I meet his gaze. He frowns, sending a nod to Pax, and another strike hits my back. Eyes stinging with unshed tears, I force my gaze over his shoulder, studying the brick wall behind him.

"If you think this is difficult, you won't like what a punishment down here entails." Mr. Bordeaux stands, letting go of my chin. "I suggest you get it right the first time." He pauses, but his feet are in a constant state of restlessness as he paces in front of me. "Is that clear?"

"Yes, Mr. Bordeaux."

I sense his smile more than see it, since I'm still studiously avoiding the vicinity of his face. "Excellent. This session has been a good start to establishing disciplined behavior." He thrusts a hand out and orders me to stand. As I slide my palm into his, I will the stiffness in my limbs to subside, but my knees give out. He keeps me upright with the strength of his grip while Pax grabs me underneath the arms until I'm steady on my feet.

Mr. Bordeaux gathers my clothing, and as I struggle into my undergarments, I feel the weight of his stare on me as tangibly as if he put his hands on me. I'm burning, and not in a good way.

"Come," he says after I finish yanking my shirt over my head. He takes me by the hand again, giving a strong pull that sends me stumbling after him. "Dinner begins in an hour. I'm sure you know by now how the chancellor disproves of tardiness."

3

My quarters in the House of Taurus are nothing like the spacious rooms I'd enjoyed during my time with Liam. The room is nondescript; a rectangle with a single mullion window at one end. Rustic plank flooring similar to the hardwood in the dungeon covers the small square footage. A twin bed takes up the space on the outer wall. Adjacent is a small bathroom with a shower—no tub, and no window either. My clothes and belongings are nowhere in sight, and even if Liam sends them, I can't imagine they'll fit into this room, considering the small closet with its sliding doors.

The space is claustrophobic and far from the luxury and comfort I'm accustomed to, but it doesn't distress me as much as Mr. Bordeaux's unbending rules.

Don't speak unless spoken to.

Don't make eye contact.

Kneel unless otherwise instructed.

More rules are bound to come, just as I'm certain I'll stumble and break them. And that's what has me wringing my hands as I pace the tiny space of my bedroom, because Heath Bordeaux terrifies me. That dungeon with all of its dark coldness and foreign equipment terrifies me.

Pax, keeper of the dungeon and master of the whip, *terrifies* me.

What happens when I screw up, and Mr. Bordeaux takes me down there for more than a "training" session? I swallow hard, but the lump of apprehension refuses to dislodge from my throat. Sliding the few hangers in the closet to the side, I search through the meager offerings and settle on a charcoal halter dress that falls to my knees. Only the thought of seeing Liam tonight makes this upcoming dinner bearable.

Except that seeing him will rip me apart. It'll be like saying goodbye all over again, only this time we'll have eleven other men for an audience.

After freshening up in the bathroom—and pulling on a pair of panties—I pace the length of the room once more, my limbs tense from nerves as the hour passes. At ten minutes till, someone knocks on the door, and a chill travels down my spine as I fall to my knees and assume the required pose. I open my mouth to call out "come in" but think better of it. I hate this uncertainty, this insecurity and fear that has me second-guessing every move.

Several tense seconds pass before the door inches open and Mr. Bordeaux's manservant enters my personal space. "Please rise. You're only required to kneel in Master Bordeaux's presence."

"Master Bordeaux?" Confusion pulls at my brows, and the question escapes before I can trap it on my tongue. The blond man overwhelming the space of my bedroom doesn't seem bothered by the question though. Unlike his employer, he doesn't appear to mind when I speak.

"Yes, though he's Mr. Bordeaux to you." He strides to the closet and chooses a pair of black heels before closing the doors I'd left open in my search of something suitable to wear. "He sent me in to prepare you for dinner," the manservant explains, holding the shoes out to me.

I rise to my feet and take the offered heels. "May I ask your name?" Too nervous to meet his eyes, I focus on the shoes, fingers tracing the swirling, glittery design. "I don't know what I should call you."

Suddenly, building a rapport with this man seems important. With my ladies exiled for the next month and Mr. Bordeaux's gag order in effect, his manservant will probably be my only form of companionship in the coming weeks.

"Of course," he says, voice lowering in sympathy as if he knows what the simplicity of his presence, and the use of my voice, might mean to me. "It's Loren."

"Is it okay if I call you Loren?"

"Yes."

"Thank you," I murmur as I slip on the shoes, grateful for at least one ally in this house, because it sure as hell isn't Loren's master.

"You're welcome." Loren holds the door open with a nod of his blond head, gesturing for me to precede him into the wide hallway that leads to the rest of Mr. Bordeaux's home. "Master Bordeaux instructed me to pass along some directions for dinner." We make our way into the main living room, with its sleek black groupings of lounges and curved chairs, crystal-accented side tables, and the grand piano on proud display in front of the wall of windows facing the ocean.

The House of Taurus is high-end with a sterile edge that leaves me cold. It's unwelcoming to Liam's inviting style that urged Faye and me to spread out sketchbooks and drawing pencils, snack trays left half-eaten on the table as we talked fashion and friendship. I can't imagine using this space for such an afternoon of freedom, especially since Mr. Bordeaux sent my ladies away the first chance he got.

Loren comes to a stop in the middle of the great room and stands at attention, hands at his back as he watches the double doors I assume lead into his master's private quarters. "After Master Bordeaux instructs you to stand, you're to follow behind him to the dining room, head bowed and hands at your back. When he's seated, you'll kneel at his side the way he taught you and wait for further instruction." Loren meets my gaze, and I'm taken aback by the near translucence of his gray eyes. They're set deep, fringed with thick black lashes, and almost colorless from the light pouring through the windows.

"Do you have any questions?" he asks.

Where do I start? I'm trying to form a reply—scrambling to grab hold of the many questions firing through my synapses—when those double doors across from us open. I drop to the floor with my heart pounding a furious rhythm in my chest.

"Did you explain the rules to her?"

"Yes, Master Bordeaux. She knows what to expect."

"Excellent." Mr. Bordeaux takes a step closer, holding out a hand. "Rise, my queen."

I do, careful not to meet his eyes. As he turns his back

to me, issuing a command to follow him, nervous energy flutters in my belly. I clasp my sweaty hands at my back and keep my head down, each obedient step taking me further away from that sterile space that is the House of Taurus and closer to the comfort of Liam's presence.

As we descend to the first floor, I can't help but speculate on what my life will be like if Mr. Bordeaux wins the auction. Will he treat me like this for the rest of my life, nothing more than an obedient slave he keeps stowed away in a closet-sized room, silenced until he lets me speak?

I'm fighting the burn of vomit in my throat when we reach the dining room. Threads of conversation hit me all at once, and I sense the eleven other men—and my ladies, who, from my peripheral, are seated in their designated chairs.

As I kneel next to Mr. Bordeaux, the din of voices falls silent, chairs scrape into place, and everyone settles in for the evening. But my world narrows only to the floor in front of me, and the man in the suit to my right.

"Why is the queen kneeling during dinner?" Liam's voice falls over me like a warm blanket.

"That is not your concern, Chancellor." Mr. Bordeaux taps his fingers on the table, the staccato hinting at his irritation.

I'm imagining the clench of Liam's jaw, the protest that wants to tumble from his beautiful mouth, when Faye's words make my muscles tense.

"The chancellor is right. She's not a dog, Mr. Bordeaux. She's a queen."

Oh God.

I spring to my feet before he can react and shoot my

oldest friend and confidant a harsh glare. "Go to your quarters. You'll spend the evening alone without dinner."

Faye's eyes widen, her expression stricken as the reprimand settles between us. I've never wielded my authority over her in such a way, always acting with deference to our friendship and the fact that Faye is more like a sister to me than a subject, but I can't allow her behavior to continue.

It's too dangerous.

Pointing to the exit, I stare her down, willing her to obey, and that's when Mr. Bordeaux rises beside me.

"You're out of line, Novalee. It's not your place to punish her. It's mine." His ire wraps around me, and I sense the scowl on his face rather than witness it because my attention fixes on Faye.

"Then I'll take her punishment. Please send her away. I beg of you."

My words send Faye scrambling from her chair, mouth twisted in outrage. "No!" Her gaze seeks Liam. "Chancellor, please do something. She's not safe with him."

I don't know how she came to that conclusion, since she's barely spent two minutes in the same room with Mr. Bordeaux, but something about him has pricked at her intuition.

She felt the same way about my uncle when he arrived six years ago.

Liam pushes a hand through his coppery hair, revealing his stressed state of mind. "Your disobedience isn't helping the queen." Pausing, his eyes narrow. "For the next month, Novalee is the subject of Mr. Bordeaux."

The man in question closes the short distance to where she stands, hands on her hips despite the sharp lines of anxiety on her face. He grabs her by the chin. "If you know what's best for your queen, you will keep your mouth shut while she takes *your* punishment. Is that clear?"

She doesn't answer at first, prompting him to shake her chin until the sought-after words fall from her lips. "Y-yes, Mr. Bordeaux."

"Kneel and don't even think of moving until it's over."

Her legs buckle, lips trembling as she mouths an apology to me from her spot on the floor.

"Loren," Mr. Bordeaux says with a snap of his fingers.

His manservant materializes from the edge of the room. "Yes, Master Bordeaux?"

"Bring me a ball gag."

He hurries away to do his master's bidding, and the room falls silent as Mr. Bordeaux reaches for his belt. "Bend over the table and lift your skirt," he commands me, sliding that thick strap of leather from around his waist. He loops it in one fist, and I know without a doubt he won't change his mind the way Liam did four days ago.

Just as I know he'll make it hurt something fierce—far worse than the bite of Pax's whip in the dungeon this afternoon. Steeling myself for what's coming, I lean over the table and lift the skirt of my dress above my buttocks, determined *not* to cry.

Because I can't let this cruel man win.

Mr. Bordeaux sets the belt on the table long enough to yank my panties to my knees, fingers rough against my skin, and my gaze clashes with Liam's. He's far from stoic, his hands fisted on the table, his mouth a severe line as he glares at the man lingering behind me.

Thighs rigid, my whole backside tingles, and I struggle to draw in a deep breath.

"If anyone in this room tries to interfere with my authority," Mr. Bordeaux says, and by the flare of Liam's nostrils I know the warning is for the chancellor, "the queen will be the one to pay for your disregard of protocol."

The color drains from Liam's face. In the month since I've known him, he's never looked so…helpless. It's an expression I can't stand on him, because it doesn't belong. He's too strong to be so flayed, vulnerability spilling from his being.

Because of me.

Because he feels the need to protect me, but coming to my defense now will only mean more punishment. Unable to confront the defeat in his brown eyes, I shift my focus to Sebastian.

And that isn't any better.

At first glance, the lion seems bored, and if it weren't for the unfailing strength of his stare, I'd think he was unaffected. Loren's return breaks the tense silence in the room, and Mr. Bordeaux pushes a rubber ball against my lips with a clipped order to open my mouth.

"You and your lady need to curb those sharp tongues," he says, forcing my lips open. He tightens the strap around my head, testing the gag to make sure it won't slip out. The contraption does more than gag me—it humiliates me on a level I didn't know existed. All eyes in the room fixate on my degradation as saliva seeps from the corners of my spread lips.

Mr. Bordeaux shifts behind me, and yet I still don't expect it; that first strike to my buttocks that stings my eyes. I blink, holding back the pain, and bite down on the gag when he hits me again.

Liam startles with each strike. After the third, he rubs his hands down his face, stricken as he stares at the place setting in front of him. He can't watch this any more than he could issue such a punishment himself.

But this is worse. The knowledge is instinctual. Liam Castle would never strike me with such force—the kind of sadism that rips apart my defenses until I'm black and blue and too close to bawling for it to stop.

And that only makes me want to smother my reaction more. It's a stubborn move, full of pride and rebellion, and part of me hopes he'll hit harder because that will mean my inaction is getting under his skin.

He can make me kneel and avoid eye contact and silence my voice, but he can't make me cry.

At some point, I detect the agony of Faye's sobs over the strikes of leather to welted skin. My fingernails gouge my palms through the clutch of the thin skirt, and I turn my head to avoid the sight of Liam's crumbling composure. That's when I realize Elise is crying, too.

And in the seat next to her, the man with the green eyes —usually crinkled at the corners with a secret smile— watches with an edge of dark fury that intrigues me. He turns to Elise, distracting her as another horrific blow assaults my backside.

He's protecting her from witnessing the worst of it, and I cling to the hope it gives me as Mr. Bordeaux metes out the last strikes, using excessive force and leaving me weak and boneless on the table.

After it's over, I return the stares of the eleven men

surrounding the table, one by one, and discover reactions ranging from horror to arousal and everything in between.

Movement sounds behind me. Light footsteps, the slide of leather against fabric, and the unmistakable clank of a belt buckle.

"Loren, return Faye to her quarters," Mr. Bordeaux says. "And deliver the queen's dinner to her, seeing as how the queen won't be able to eat with her mouth gagged."

Faye lets loose one last sob, and a strangled, "I'm sorry."

And then she's gone, and I ache at the thought of not seeing her again for a whole month, of not being able to tell her how sorry I am for the harsh way I spoke to her.

"Need I remind you of your place, my queen?"

I let my skirt fall to my knees, covering my punished ass, then yank my panties up. With a stifled groan of agony, I lower to my haunches. Mr. Bordeaux reclaims his seat, and dinner begins, the aroma of spicy beef shooting hunger pangs through my belly since I haven't eaten since breakfast.

Is this part of his punishment—forced fasting? Even more disturbing is the thought he has the power to flat out starve me for the next month if I don't please him.

I'm alone in this, unable to ask for help or leniency. This sadistic man at my side might break me before the month is up, and there's nothing I can do about it, short of doing something stupid, like trying to escape.

Or towing his line.

And right then I realize where my power lies—in obedience.

Complete and utter, without question, obedience. The rebellious girl in me revolts, claws out and ears steaming with indignant anger. But the smart girl in me knows how to survive.

Halfway through the main course, Mr. Bordeaux calls for Loren again, and the manservant hands his master a velvet bag with a drawstring closure.

"My gift to the queen," Mr. Bordeaux says, grabbing my attention as he tips the bag and dumps several diamonds onto the table in front of me.

Twelve of them, I'm guessing, and a quick count confirms my assessment.

"As you all know, I'm having her crown designed. These diamonds will go into the final setting...assuming she gets to keep them all." He scoots in his seat and takes me by the chin, and I stare over his shoulder at the white dinnerware, avoiding eye contact.

"For each transgression you make, my queen, I will take away a diamond." He pauses, the unwavering weight of his stare making my face flush. "Earning it back will be painful and degrading."

A collective murmur travels around the table, until Mr. Green Eyes to the left of me—from the House of Gemini—speaks up. "What the hell is wrong with you? You can't hold her gift over her head like that."

"I can and I will. It's my gift to give," he says, tone soft as his thumb rubs the line of my jaw, "and that means it's mine to take away."

4

The morning after the dinner with the Brotherhood, Mr. Bordeaux went away on a business trip, leaving Loren to give me a proper tour in his absence.

"You'll help with meal prep," he says, showing me around the massive kitchen with its ivory cabinetry and gleaming quartz countertops. He opens several drawers and cupboards, pointing out where to find everything from pots and pans to spices. "Master Bordeaux doesn't eat until lunchtime, so your kitchen duties won't start until eleven."

We stop at the center island, and Loren goes over the menu for the coming week before touching on my cleaning duties. "After lunch prep, you'll do some light housekeeping until it's time to prepare for dinner." He pauses, assessing me. "Do you have experience with any of this?"

"Domestic tasks weren't high on my uncle's list of priorities."

Because he taught me to behave like an obedient queen —not an obedient servant. But I don't share that thought with Loren for fear of sounding like an elitist brat.

"That's understandable. The good news is with Master Bordeaux gone for the next few days, you'll have plenty of time to practice some skills in the kitchen."

"Does he go away on business often?" I ask as Loren shows me an adjacent supply closet five times bigger than the wardrobe in my room.

"Twice a month, sometimes more when luck favors him."

According to Loren, Mr. Bordeaux buys and sells precious stones at auction, and with that knowledge I send out a prayer that my keeper will be especially prosperous in his hunt, requiring frequent trips during the coming weeks.

We come upon a set of double doors, and Loren uses his master key to let us inside. "This room is off-limits unless I allow you in here to clean."

The space is a cavernous vault of fine art and jewelry displays, but the life-sized paintings of gorgeous women wearing nothing but precious stones draw my focus.

"Who are these women?" I ask before thinking the question through. My cheeks burn with embarrassment at my forwardness.

"They're models Mr. Bordeaux hired to wear his rarest acquisitions."

The poses are similar and surprisingly tasteful, featuring women lounging in chairs, their legs crossed and long hair cascading over their breasts—a real life canvas for sparkling jewels.

I zero in on the initials in the bottom right-hand corner of each portrait. "SAS?" I ask.

"Sebastian Stone, from the House of Leo. You'll have to ask him what the middle initial stands for," Loren says, gesturing at the painting. "He does all of Master Bordeaux's portraits."

Sexy as sin comes to mind when thinking of what those initials stand for.

Just the thought of Sebastian sends a warm tingle down my back, and I wonder what it would be like to sit before him like the women in the paintings, sensual and seductive?

The idea isn't unpleasant.

Loren ushers me out of the forbidden room that houses Mr. Bordeaux's collection, and we continue the tour as he gives me a crash course on daily chores.

"Can I ask you something, Loren?"

We come full circle in the great room, and he stalls, sensuous lips sliding into a frown. "You aren't required to silence your voice with me. You can ask me anything."

"Am I allowed to leave the residence? You know...to go outside or to the library on the first floor?"

A glint of sympathy passes through his eyes. "Unfortunately, no. Master Bordeaux requires that you stay in your quarters when you're not busy with chores."

"Why?" The strained tone of my voice gives away my despair. "Does he hate me?"

Taking my hand, Loren leads me to a leather couch, and we sit together, side by side. He doesn't let go of my hand. "Master Bordeaux is a very demanding and complicated man. He has no reason to hate you, but you'll have to earn his trust and respect before he gives back the liberties we all take for granted."

"Like the freedom to go outside?" I wince at my caustic tone.

Instead of taking offense, the dry question makes Loren smile. "It's the little things in life we miss, isn't it?"

"Do you mind if I ask why you work for him?"

Loren contemplates whether to answer—I can pinpoint the second his openness shuts down and he withdraws, letting my hand slip out of his.

"I'm sorry," I say, backing away from that thread of conversation. "It's none of my business."

"It's okay. Master Bordeaux wants the two of us to get to know each other." He clears his throat, and I can't tell if he's nervous, or suffering from a sudden case of springtime allergies. "So it's important you know I don't work for him. He's my master in every sense of the word, Novalee."

"I don't understand."

"I serve and obey him, and in return, he takes care of me." Loren stands. "In time, you'll understand." He holds out a hand, urging me to follow his lead. "But we've only got a few days before he returns, so how about we start in the kitchen and I teach you a few basics?"

5

Six days later, Mr. Bordeaux still hasn't returned, and I can't say I miss the man with all of his unbending rules. Embracing the solitude, I've excelled at scrubbing floors, dusting antiques and jewels that would feed a starving nation, and learning which knives to use for which vegetables—and which ones to avoid if I don't want to cut myself again.

My role in the House of Taurus is little more than a maid without compensation, but I don't mind the busy work. The meal prep and house cleaning keep me distracted, and though I've never scrubbed a toilet a day in my life, doing so now gives me a sense of calmness, left alone to the task with no one to answer to but the gleaming porcelain beneath my hands.

"You're quite the quick study."

At the sound of Mr. Bordeaux's voice, I scramble into position on my knees, bleach-scented palms facing up on my thighs. The cutoff jeans I put on for chores are frayed, pockets peeking out beneath my hands. They were among the few belongings he allowed Liam to send. My keeper chose to put the rest of my clothing collection in storage until the next man in charge decides whether to give my things to me.

"Loren says you've been settling in well during my absence. I've been pleased with his progress reports on your behavior." As he steps into the main guest bathroom, his shiny black shoes coming into view, I remain silent. "When I praise you, my queen, I expect you to respond."

"Thank you, Mr. Bordeaux."

"You're welcome." He leans down and runs a hand over my tangled locks. "You need to shower and dress for company. Come to the great room in twenty minutes." Without another word, he pivots and disappears into the hall.

Bewildered by his abrupt summons, I abandon the task, tossing the sudsy sponge into the trashcan, and hurry into my private bath, where I take a five-minute shower before pulling on a black linen dress. By the time I walk into the great room with three minutes to spare, damp hair braided on the side, my heart rate is pumping double time because his "company" can't be a good thing.

But then my eyes meet Liam's from across the room, and my pulse speeds up for a different reason. I freeze for a few seconds until the sight of Mr. Bordeaux, standing tall at Liam's side, sends me to my knees.

My stoic keeper holds up a hand, halting my descent to the floor. "The chancellor is here to join us for lunch. He's requested you not kneel during his visit."

Liam doesn't take his eyes off of me. "I also ask that you allow her freedom of speech."

"That isn't necessary, Chancellor. We have important matters to discuss and don't need the distraction of a woman's inconsequential chatter."

I bite back a retort, knowing he'll only punish me for my "sharp" tongue, and I'm not fond of the taste of rubber. Though part of me wants to know how it's possible for a woman to have a sharp tongue while being prone to mindless chatter. The two aren't complementary traits.

"Shall we?" Mr. Bordeaux says, gesturing for the chancellor to precede him into the formal dining room. I follow on their tail, and after the three of us take our seats, Liam across from me and Mr. Bordeaux at the head of the table, Loren appears with the fresh greens I prepped an hour ago. His stare is discreet as he piles lettuce and salad toppings onto each of our plates, but I detect a hint of speculation in his gray eyes.

I've only been a subject of Mr. Bordeaux's for a week, most of which he spent away on business, but sitting in a chair next to him during mealtime—instead of eating with Loren in the kitchen—feels foreign and somehow *wrong*. If it weren't for Liam's presence, I'd rather be in the kitchen with Loren.

"You said you wanted to discuss the Heart of the Queen," Mr. Bordeaux says, breaking the silence as I pick at the leafy greens on my plate.

"Yes." Liam darts his gaze in my direction. "I'm ready to sell."

I have no idea what they're talking about. My attention swings to Mr. Bordeaux as he takes a sip of wine, the motion nonchalant except for the harsh grip of his fingers on the glass.

"You surprise me, Chancellor." He sets the wineglass down, tongue darting across his lower lip. "What changed your mind?"

"I guess you can say my priorities have shifted." Liam's answer draws my gaze back to him. "I'll accept your previous offer if you grant me weekly chess sessions with Novalee."

"You're willing to part with the Heart of the Queen for a few games of chess?" Skepticism laces Mr. Bordeaux's tone.

"Yes, along with the twenty million you agreed to pay the last time you put the offer on the table."

"Where will these *sessions* take place?"

"In my penthouse."

"Absolutely not. The library will do for a game of chess."

"Fine," the chancellor says through gritted teeth. "But I want permission to touch her."

The room falls quiet as the two men stare each other down. I hold my breath, afraid to move.

Because the thought of being in Liam's arms again so soon has me on the edge of my seat, antsy with hopeful excitement.

"You seem to care a great deal about our lovely queen."

"Don't you?" Liam challenges with an arch of his brow.

The strength of Mr. Bordeaux's stare touches on me like an appraisal, as if he's calculating my worth in the ten long seconds he takes to reply to the chancellor.

"She's proven her obedience." From the corner of my eye, I spy the edge of his mouth curl. "And apparently her value."

"Do we have a deal, then?" Liam presses, voice bold

except for the small waver I'm hoping the man sitting at the head of the table doesn't notice.

"Bi-weekly sessions and ten percent off the price."

"Five percent," Liam counters.

"Seven percent." A lengthy pause ratchets the tension. "And no sexual contact."

A telling tick goes off in Liam's jaw. He wants the physical connection between us as badly as I do. "No deal, Heath. At a minimum, I require permission to kiss her."

"Desperation does *not* suit you, Chancellor."

Liam's brows narrow. "Don't mistake my affection for desperation."

"I stand corrected. Bi-weekly sessions it is, kissing allowed. Do we have a deal?"

"I'll accept your terms if you give me twenty minutes alone with Novalee first."

A pause of silence, and then hope pumps through my veins as Mr. Bordeaux stands, his chair sliding soundlessly across the floor. "Come find me when you're finished." He exits with the same brusqueness I'm coming to expect from him.

If I thought the tension was thick before, it's nothing compared to the sexual haze that falls over the dining table, food forgotten, as soon as the door shutters us in relative privacy.

Liam and I drink in the sight of each other for what feels like the first half of our twenty minutes, when in reality not even five seconds sneak by. A grandfather clock chaperones from its unobtrusive corner of the room, and I listen to the hands swing back and forth.

"What is the Heart of the Queen?" I ask, fracturing the quiet.

His attention lowers to my mouth, thoughts blatant as he folds his hands on the table—as if he wants to touch me but knows he can't. "It's a rare diamond necklace passed down the Castle line. Evangeline gave it to her eldest son before he married his queen."

His explanation whirls in my mind, and I struggle to keep up, to grasp onto the meaning behind those telling words. "So this necklace...it's a family heirloom?"

"Yes."

"I don't understand." Offending him is the last thing I want to do, but I can't help but question the wisdom in the deal he just made with my keeper. "Why would you sell it to Mr. Bordeaux for two chess games?"

"Because, my sweet inquisitive girl..." His smile is the only sign he picked up on the subtle incredulity in my tone. "You're worth it."

I haven't heard him speak the endearment since the morning I left his penthouse, but now it washes over me with the comfort of sunshine, enfolding me in a warm spring breeze, and I ache to hear him say it again. "It's just chess," I whisper, rather stupidly, because we both know he's not selling just to play a game with me.

It's true he's bartering for time with me, and he's willing to sell something undeniably valuable to get it—the kind of *valuable* you can't put a price tag on—but there has to be more to this than he's shared.

Because it doesn't make sense.

"Novalee," he says, leaning forward and fisting his hands between us. Frustration vibrates off him. "This isn't about chess. I need to see you—as often as is possible—but the money I get for the necklace is more important than I can tell you. I don't think I need to explain the extent of Heath's wealth. Out of the twelve of us, his net worth is at the top."

"Meaning he has the means to win the auction."

"Yes, he does."

"So what do you need the money for? Surely it won't be enough to outbid him."

"You're correct." Clearing his throat, he pushes his chair back and rises.

And that's when I realize he's not going to elaborate on his plans. Whatever his reasoning, he's keeping it close to his chest.

"I won't tell anyone," I point out, a little hurt that he won't let me in on the secret.

"I know you won't. I trust you, but I won't put you in a position where the knowledge can be used against you."

"Used against me how?"

"I'm assuming you've been to the dungeon?"

I stiffen in my seat. "Yes."

"If Heath catches wind that I have ulterior motives for selling, he might interrogate you for answers." Worry pinches his mouth. "In fact, I shouldn't have asked for these twenty minutes. The less you know the better."

"You're still protecting me."

"Always, my sweet girl."

"What's so special about me?"

His gaze burns through me. "I fell for you the instant I saw you."

"In the library," I whisper, remembering that day and

the complex emotions he inspired in me as the taste of him lingered on my tongue.

"No, the day my father secured your hand in marriage to the Brotherhood. You were a vision even at twelve."

"You were intimidating but memorable." I peek at him from under my lashes, worried he'll see too much in my expression because he wasn't the only boy that day to leave a lasting impression.

Even during my most intimate moments with Liam, Sebastian hovers between us, unbidden and unspoken. Someday the three of us will come to a head, and I can't help but wonder if we'll survive.

"How is Heath treating you?" he asks, breaking through the chaos in my head.

"He's very...rigid."

"Has he hurt you?"

"No, nothing too horrible."

"Has he...?" With a hard swallow, Liam drags his hand through his copper hair. "Has he touched you yet?"

"No." Biting my lip, I brush my thumb across the giant diamond ring Liam put on my finger last month. "He's been gone all week, but he doesn't seem interested in...that."

Some of the tension drains from his features. "That's not surprising. Some of us have theories."

My brows furrow. "What do you mean?"

"It's not for me to say." With a glance at his watch, he rounds the table. "Just obey him and you'll get through the rest of the month without too much trauma."

"And what about next month, Liam?" Fear shakes the accusing words from my lips as I rise to face him on solid ground. "This doesn't end when I leave the House of Taurus."

His nearness heats my body without him laying a finger on me. "The House of Gemini will be easier. Landon is a decent guy."

My instincts told me as much, but I'm relieved to hear him confirm it. "I miss you," I say despite the ache in my throat. I tilt my head and meet his warm gaze. "So much, and it's only been a week."

"The feeling is mutual." He leans forward, and his mouth teases the edge of mine. "I want you naked in my arms, those sexy legs wrapped around me in bed."

"He didn't say you couldn't kiss me today," I whisper, my exhales mixing with his.

"He didn't give me permission either." Shuttering his eyes, he takes a step back, and disappointment knifes through my gut. "I can't risk it, Novalee. No matter how much I want to."

I want to launch myself into his arms and beg him to never let me go. The urge is inescapable, and I suck in several deep breaths to quell it.

Because I understand his position. A few moments of bliss isn't worth a lifetime of servitude with someone like Mr. Bordeaux.

"Can I ask a favor?" I say, clinging to a much needed change of subject.

"Of course."

"Will you check on my ladies? Mr. Bordeaux won't let me see them."

"It's already done. I checked on them the day after the

dinner. Faye profusely apologized for her behavior that night."

"So they're okay?"

"Yes." He studies me, eyes narrowed. "They're worried about you, as am I."

"I'm fine."

He says nothing at first. "Would you tell me if you weren't?"

"Yes…maybe." I pause, swallowing hard. "I guess it would depend."

"On what?"

"On whether telling you would be futile."

Neither of us voice the elephant taking up half the space in the dining room.

Because Liam's as powerless as I am in the House of Taurus.

6

As a reward for my good behavior since he returned home a week ago, Mr. Bordeaux let me venture outside. Such a basic privilege, a simple joy I'd always taken for granted until I could do it no more. Walking along the edge of the cliffs, I close my eyes against the crisp breeze, hoping to find a hint of serenity.

Because I miss the sunshine and warmth of home. The endless azure skies and the fragrant comfort of plumeria.

I miss *my* home.

Zodiac Island is but a barren rock—a beautiful, majestic cliff overlooking the sea. Wind whips my hair around my head, arranging my braids with Mother Nature's powerful hand. Springtime doesn't exist in this place. The northern location means there's nothing but dreary skies and a freezing windchill strong enough to ice over hell, and yet...I find something undeniably magical about this spot on the edge of the world.

I wish I hated it more. I wish I hated it less.

I wish time would go by faster. I'm only halfway into my

month with Mr. Bordeaux, but the days pass at an agonizing pace. The only highlight of this day is that I'll see Liam later for a game of chess. If not for the bitter chill, I'd stay outside the walls of the estate until my session with the chancellor, clinging to the heady sense of freedom. Instead, I return inside and take the elevator to Mr. Bordeaux's floor in silent contemplation.

Because he gave me an afternoon of unequivocal freedom, but I'm returning to my prison, of my own free will, and that makes me question my sanity. Am I so lost that I can't enjoy an afternoon without someone telling me what to do? Shaking the disturbing thought from my head, I enter through the main door, distracted with thoughts of curling up with a good book, but odd sounds halt me on the threshold of my bedroom.

Grunting.

Rhythmic and fast-paced.

Groans.

Coming from Mr. Bordeaux's quarters at the end of the wide hallway. I spy the ajar door, and the sounds filtering out draw me closer to peek through the crack.

I wish I hadn't.

Because Mr. Bordeaux isn't alone. Loren is with him, and the two are a tangle of limbs on the humongous bed, bodies rutting, skin covered in sweat.

I'm not supposed to see this.

It must be the reason he sent me away for the afternoon. He believes I'm outside enjoying my freedom, grateful for his permission to leave the residence for a few hours.

Instead, I'm spying on him while he pounds his manservant from behind. Loren turns his head, his hooded gray eyes latching onto mine, and we both gasp, drawing the attention of his master. I duck out of sight, but the tremble in my legs and the furious pace of my heart know better.

It's too late.

The door swings all the way open behind me, and I drop to my knees, hands shaking on my thighs as his feet stomp closer. He appears in front of me, naked and vibrating with anger.

"I-I'm s-sorry, Mr. Bordeaux."

"Did I give you permission to speak?"

I open my mouth to reply, but fear imprisons my vocal cords.

"Answer me!" His voice booms off the walls, making me jump.

"N-no, Mr. Bordeaux."

"Did I give you permission to spy on me in my private quarters?"

"No, Mr. Bordeaux."

"Then why were you doing just that?"

Scared to say the wrong thing, I lick my lips to buy a couple of seconds. "It was cold outside, so I c-came in and h-heard noises..."

"And instead of returning to your quarters where you belong, you stuck your nose in my private business, is that the sum of it, Novalee?"

"Yes, Mr. Bordeaux. I'm sorry."

"You will certainly be apologetic later, because your actions have cost you a diamond."

Oh God.

I blink back tears. He's going to take away my session

with Liam. The certainty of it fists my heart, squeezing until I can't breathe.

Because I *need* this time with Liam—it's the only thing giving me hope since I saw him at lunch a week ago. Before I can question the wisdom of my actions, I raise my hand, dying to ask Mr. Bordeaux if he's going to take away the visit.

"Would you like permission to speak, my queen?"

"Yes, Mr. Bordeaux."

"Permission is denied. Go to your quarters and wait for me on your knees."

I scramble to do his bidding, exhaling a harrowing breath as I shut myself away in my bedroom. Lowering to my knees to wait isn't an issue—I fall to them, composure wrecked as the tears I held back minutes ago drench my face.

He doesn't make me wait long, and I'm not sure if that's a blessing, or a curse. Mr. Bordeaux appears in the doorway dressed in dark gray slacks, erection straining behind his zipper. He shuts the door, enclosing us inside my room, and his presence is too imposing for the cramped space. Each inhale and exhale from his mouth seems to steal all the air.

Or maybe I'm just holding my breath, as if not breathing will delay the inevitable.

"You have two options to earn back your diamond." Bending, he grips my chin hard, and I feel his eyes on me, challenging me to return his gaze.

I *want* to lock my eyes with his in defiance. Maybe doing so would mean holding on to my last shred of self-respect, despite the consequences it'll bring. Because I'm disgusted with this man and his sick games, and even more disgusted with my inaction.

But I want to see Liam more, so I study the wall over Mr. Bordeaux's shoulder, my face burning under his perusal—a dangerous cocktail of revulsion and rage.

"Option number one," he says, letting his hand fall from my chin. "Tell the chancellor you willingly relinquish your visit with him today. No rescheduling. You'll have to wait another two weeks for your little chess game." Returning to his full height, he pulls something out of his pocket and dangles it in front of my face. "Or there's option two."

My gaze stalls on the contraption in his hand. It reminds me of the gag he used at the dinner with the Brotherhood, only this one doesn't have a rubber ball; it has a metal ring attached to two leather straps that buckle. I swallow hard as he swings it back and forth in front of me.

"Do you know what this is?"

I shake my head. "Not exactly, Mr. Bordeaux."

"It's a gag that will force your mouth open to be used in whatever way I see fit." Letting a beat pass, he takes an unhurried stroll to the twin bed and back. "I'll tie your hands behind you so you won't be able to remove the gag. You'll have zero control, and the punishment ends when I say it does. This is option two, my queen. Accept it and I'll allow you to see the chancellor today."

The thought of wearing that gag and taking his cock makes me sick, but it could be worse. If I've learned anything about the opposite sex and the appendage between their legs, it's that a woman has great power between her lips, in more ways than one.

I'll make him come, and then it'll be over. I raise my hand without questioning my decision.

"You may speak."

"I'll take the second option, Mr. Bordeaux."

"I thought you might." A hint of a smug smile infuses his words, and for a second I wonder if I made the right choice. A pang of dread goes off in my belly.

He doesn't give me time to doubt myself. With one hand fisting my hair, he forces my mouth open and inserts the metal ring before tightening the straps around my head. The contraption is snug between my lips, stretching them wide open, the fit rendering the gag impossible to dislodge.

He removes his belt, and I give a protesting whine when he reaches for me. Instead of striking me with the pliable strap, he uses the belt to restrain my hands behind me.

"Stick out your tongue," he orders, digging into his pocket once more, this time revealing a chain.

Unable to make out what's attached to the end, I dart my tongue out with trepidation. He presses something between his thumb and forefinger, and the cool sensation of metal on my tongue makes me flinch. The thing clamps onto the center like a vise, causing an intense pain where the prongs press into my tongue. With a sharp cry, I jerk back, but the more I fight it, the more acute the pain becomes.

He stands, fisting the chain and keeping my mouth level with his erection, and I watch in agony as he exposes his cock.

"You interrupted something you shouldn't have seen." With firm, measured strokes, he pumps his shaft, aiming the tip at my clamped tongue. "You deprived Loren of receiving the gift of my cum, so now I'm going to finish all over your face, and there isn't a thing you can do to stop it." He forces my tongue out as far as it'll go, making my eyes bleed tears from the increased pressure.

His breaths come fast and heavy, and with several more wet strokes of his cock, he erupts. I close my eyes as his salty release spurts onto my tongue. He grunts, and another stream of thick fluid hits my eyelids and cheeks.

Mr. Bordeaux wipes it from my eyes, smearing it into my cheeks and hair. "You're going to meet the chancellor wearing my cum." He jerks the chain again, and my lids fly open.

Suddenly, I'm staring into the cool hazel eyes of my keeper.

"What did I say about eye contact?" A rhetorical question, since he's still got my tongue in a vise. The mean line of his mouth sends my attention to his thighs.

He gives another tug, this time with an order to stand, and I stumble into him. One hand fisting my hair, the other yanking on that evil chain until my tears trail over cum-caked cheeks, he forces me to my feet. "Look at me," he seethes.

My watery eyes meet his again.

"If you breathe a word of what you saw to *anyone*," he says, pulling on the chain until I let out a high-pitched cry, "I'll cut out your goddamn tongue."

Nausea rises, and I'm powerless to swallow it down. All I can do is breathe through my nose until it subsides.

"Blink three times if you understand."

I flutter my lashes, and he lets go of the chain long enough to zip up his pants. But the relief is short-lived, because he's herding me out of my bedroom by the tongue. We leave through the main doors, and the elevator ride to the first floor passes in a distressed blur. I know where we're going, but I don't want to accept it, because the thought of Liam witnessing my degradation is more than I can bear.

My face is a mess of tears and cum, hair hanging into my eyes, which I welcome because I can't meet Liam's gaze anyway. The door to the library slams shut behind us.

"I apologize for the tardiness," Mr. Bordeaux says. "I had to take care of an issue." He removes the clamp, and I whimper at the flood of pain that hits my tongue all at once.

"What's going on?" Liam demands as my keeper unties my hands and unbuckles the straps around my head. I feel the weight of his curiosity on me, like bricks pressing me into the floor, and I wish the marble under my feet would fissure and suck me through the cracks.

"She's all yours, Chancellor." Mr. Bordeaux exits the library, leaving me utterly humiliated.

7

The musky scent of Mr. Bordeaux wafts between us in the silence, an insurmountable wall that failed to disappear with the exit of my keeper. Rubbing the ache from my jaw, I avoid Liam's stricken expression.

"What happened?" He reaches for me, and my first instinct is to push him away.

"Don't. He's all over me."

"What do you mean?"

"He came on my face."

With a shaky breath, Liam slides a hand along my cheek, unmindful of another man's claim on my skin. "It's no secret I have to share you." He runs a thumb across my lower lip. "Are you okay?"

"I'm fine."

"There's that phrase again." His fingers graze the leftover stickiness on my cheek. "Did he hurt you?"

Only my pride.

"He humiliated me," I say instead, remembering how he hauled me through the estate by the chain latched to my tongue. My only comfort is that no one else witnessed the degrading parade.

"Are you going to tell me why he punished you?"

I shake my head. "I can't."

He frowns. "Is this an issue of futility?"

It's an issue of me wanting to keep my tongue.

"Tattling will only get me into more trouble. It's over now."

A tick goes off in Liam's jaw. "Do you believe you deserved what he did?"

"He's not like you, Liam. When you punish, you do it with compassion. What he did...no one deserves that."

"Then don't let shame rule your emotions, Novalee. You have no control over how the Brotherhood treats you." Slowly, he backs me toward the door until my spine meets the wood. "Just like you can't stop me from kissing the hell out of you right now." Stepping forward, he closes the last few inches, bringing our bodies flush with each other.

"Isn't this against the rules?" I meet his gaze, reeled in by the lure of those deep umber depths.

"He gave me permission to kiss you, so that's what I'm going to do."

I lift a finger to his descending mouth. "Please don't."

"Why, my sweet girl?"

"Because I'm a mess."

"His scent isn't a claim on you, but my mouth will be, and I'll be damned if I let him ruin this moment." His lips silence any further protest, his tongue seeking entrance, and I forget all about Mr. Bordeaux and his rules. The monster's ejaculation on my face ceases to matter when Liam kisses me like this—with ardent urgency, his lips possessive and tongue combative, pummeling me into sweet surrender.

Clutching the lapels of his jacket, I groan into his mouth. "Please," I breathe against his lips.

"What are you pleading for?"

"Don't make me go back to him." Inching away, I meet his eyes. "Let's run away. I know you have the means, and I have money in a trust my uncle can't touch. It's mine when I turn twenty-one. We can have a life together."

Framing my face between his hands, he gives me a sad smile. "This is my home." With a hard swallow, he lets a beat pass. "It's my duty to carry out my family's legacy. But I can offer you a promise," he says, entwining our fingers. "I'll do everything in my power to make sure we have a life together."

"How can you be so confident?"

"I have faith."

"I don't know if I can make it through the next several months. I've still got two weeks with Mr. Bordeaux, and in September, Pax will have his turn."

He winces, as if he knows exactly what I'm talking about, because it's obvious the keeper of the dungeon is a psychotic sadist.

"Pax won't be a problem."

"How can you say that? You have limited power as the chancellor, remember?"

"I'm aware of my finite capabilities, but my brothers often underestimate me. I need you to trust me on this. Can you do that?"

"I can try."

"It's a start," he murmurs, grabbing my hand and pulling

me further into the library. I spot a game of chess on the table where, six weeks ago, a contract awarding my life to the Brotherhood awaited my uncle's signature.

That first day within these walls seems like a lifetime ago.

"I'll give you the first move," he says, gesturing toward the side with the white pieces.

I slide into the seat, and after he settles in across from me, I push a pawn forward. "Ladies first, is that it? We both know you're going to win."

"How about I let you have this one so I can get back to worshipping your mouth?" He follows my lead and moves a pawn, but his attention stalls on my lips.

My heart skips a beat. "That sounds tempting, but when the day comes that I *do* beat you, I don't want there to be any question of your defeat." I slide a bishop out, eyes locked on his from across the table.

"I can respect that." A grin threatens at the corner of his lips.

Several moments sneak by as he contemplates his next move, and my mind wanders to what I saw in Mr. Bordeaux's private quarters. My keeper's relationship with Loren is something he's obviously hiding, but is it because he's protecting himself, or the manservant?

And from who? His parents?

Sebastian admitted he's under a lot of pressure from his family to marry me, and I imagine that is also true for the other members of the Brotherhood. Is that why Mr. Bordeaux wants to win the auction?

Because he needs a wife to cover the truth?

"The wheels are spinning over there, but I highly doubt

you have chess on the mind." Liam shoots me a speculative look as he pushes another pawn forward.

"I was just wondering about your parents," I say, sticking with part of the truth, at least. "I've met none of the Brotherhood's family, other than your father when I was twelve. Do they ever come to the estate to visit?"

"Not during the first year. The new Brotherhood needs time to settle in without the influence of legacy members. I guess you might call their absence a tradition."

"So you don't see your parents at all?"

"Not until after the auction, but we do keep in contact via phone and email."

"You must miss your family." A pang shoots through my chest, and I suck in a breath and hold it for several seconds to staunch the ache threatening to creep in. "A day doesn't pass that I don't miss my parents."

His expression softens, the furrow between his brows smoothing out in sympathy. "I don't think I ever told you how sorry I am for what happened to your parents. You were so young."

"I miss them." I swallow past the lump in my throat. "Sometimes I think I see them—my mother, especially. It happens at odd times. I'll come around a corner and think I see her sitting at the kitchen table, scribbling in her journal and sampling the baked goods the chef made for the day. Other times, I can almost imagine my father behind his desk, papers piled high in front of him."

"They'll always be with you, Novalee." He reaches across the table and takes my hand, and I wonder if that simple gesture of comfort and companionship go against the rules.

As his warm fingers entwine with mine, I can't bring myself to care.

If I could visit Faye or Elise, they would hug me and offer their shoulders to lean on. But they aren't here. Liam is, and he cares enough about me to *want* to give comfort. If I didn't love him before, I do now.

"Your move, my sweet girl." Giving one last squeeze of my hand, he lets go, and my attention returns to the board.

But my heart isn't into winning. Because he's right—the sooner the game's over, the sooner I can feel his mouth on mine again. Recklessly, I move my queen into the path of his castle.

Liam shakes his head. "I thought you wanted a fair game?"

"I guess I want you to kiss me more."

His hand halts above the conquering piece, and he watches me intently, his hot gaze an ember that flares brighter than the sun. The rope of tension snaps between us. Abandoning the game, he scoots his chair back with a crook of his finger.

I round the table, and he reaches for me—or I reach for him. All I know is I'm in heaven astride his lap, knees tucked on either side of his hips as our mouths fuse. He groans into the kiss, his cock expanding between us, hard and long against the zipper of his slacks.

"When I get inside you for the first time," he says, burying his face in my shoulder, "I'll never want to leave."

My core clenches, hot and snug against his cock, and I grind against him to inspire that gruff sound in the back of his throat again.

"Jesus, Novalee. We're crossing a line here. You need to get up."

"No." I infuse my tone with pure defiance, tilting my hips once more, and he groans again.

"You think you can defy me because I can't lay my hand on your ass? Is that it?"

"I want your hand on my ass."

"You know it's not allowed. But I can still punish you." He yanks my hair, pulling my head back until our eyes meet. "I can cancel our next visit."

"No!" I scramble off his lap, hurt that he'd even think to do that.

He rises with a glint of predatory glee and stalks toward me. "You think you don't have to obey me because you belong to him for the month?"

"I...Liam, no."

He takes me by the chin, his fingers gentle. "You're still mine as much as you are his, so the next time I tell you to remove your tempting little body from the vicinity of my cock, do not tell me no."

My gaze falls to his chest. "I'm sorry."

"You're forgiven." He presses his lips to mine, lingering with urgency. "Our time is up, my sweet girl. It's time for me to escort you back to your quarters."

8

Thankfully, my keeper is absent, locked away in his study on a conference call. Before dinner prep, I take a shower, turning up the water temperature as hot as I can stand, and wash the degradation of Mr. Bordeaux's punishment off my skin. After dinner, I spend the rest of the evening alone in my room, curled up in front of the mullion window with a book about a shapeshifting dragon as the sun kisses the horizon.

Half past nine, a knock sounds on the door. I sit up, set my book aside, and call for Loren to come in because he's the only one who gives me the courtesy of knocking. Mr. Bordeaux never announces his presence, choosing instead to barge in whenever he pleases and expecting me to fall to my knees, regardless of whether I'm decent.

"I'm sorry to disturb you," Loren says after closing the door behind him. He takes a spot on the other end of my bed and stares out the window at the twilight mural streaking across the sky. "You were quiet during dinner."

"I guess I'm still processing." I shift on the mattress,

drawing my feet underneath me, and take in the pensive slant of his mouth.

"What you saw today..." With a jittery sigh, he meets my gaze. "Does it change how you look at me?"

"What?" The word comes out sharp with surprise. "Why would it?"

"Because you barely said two words to me during dinner."

"I was upset, Loren." Tentatively, I place my hand on his arm. "Not at you, but at *him*. He threatened to cut out my tongue if I told anyone."

His brows furrow over stormy eyes. "He's very protective of me. And what you saw...it opens old wounds."

"How so?"

"Did you know we went to college together?"

I shake my head.

"We became very close, and when my father found out, he went ballistic." Hurt bathes his face at the memory. "He said he'd rather see me dead than with a man."

"How did he find out?"

"The same way you did."

My heart aches for him. "I'm so sorry, Loren."

"My father couldn't accept it. He threatened to disown me if I didn't stay away from Master Bordeaux." Crossing his arms, he lowers his head. "So I told him to cut me off, and Master Bordeaux took me in as his employee."

"But he's much more than that," I say, softening my tone, "isn't he?"

"Yes."

Several seconds go by as I consider asking what's on my

mind. "Why does he want to keep your relationship a secret?"

"If his parents find out, they'll make sure I disappear from his life."

My eyes widen. "Disappear how?"

"Have me banished from the island. The legacy members of the Brotherhood are too powerful to go up against."

"Does Mr. Bordeaux know you're here confiding in me?"

"He sent me in to talk to you."

"Isn't he worried I'll tell someone?" Though I have no plans to, since I want to keep my tongue. A huge part of me is certain Mr. Bordeaux will follow through on his threat if I dare speak of what I walked in on today.

"My banishment will accomplish nothing. It won't negate his need for an heir. It's in your best interest to keep this secret."

His words sink in, weighing down my spirit because if the House of Taurus wins my hand in marriage, it won't be a partnership.

I'll be the third wheel in a secret affair, only worthy because of my uterus and my status as Mr. Bordeaux's wife.

"Does anyone else know about the two of you?" I ask, remembering Liam's comment about having theories.

"The chancellor might have his suspicions, but no one else has given thought to the possibility." Clearing his throat, he rises, failing to hide a wince as he steps toward the door.

"Are you okay?" Concern has me on my feet.

"I'm fine."

There's that phrase again.

Liam's words echo through my head, and I know Loren isn't *fine*.

"What did he do to you?" I ask, following him to the door.

"Nothing I didn't deserve." He turns, expression brimming with self-loathing. "I'm the one who left the door open. If not for my mistake, you wouldn't have seen what you did, and he wouldn't have punished you for it."

As he reaches for the doorknob, I grab his arm to stop him. "You deserve better than him." As far as I can tell, banishment from Zodiac Island would be a blessing.

"He's strict and uncompromising, but you haven't met his generous, kind side yet. You don't know him like I do."

After everything Mr. Bordeaux has put me through, I have no desire to.

9

Since the night he came to my bedroom to confide in me, Loren and I fall into our normal routine of shared duties mixed with moments of conversation that verge on friendship. Mr. Bordeaux is especially busy, even going away for a few days on an acquisition trip.

A rare ruby, or so Loren tells me.

I can't say I'm heartbroken by my keeper's absence, or how quickly the days seem to pass with him gone. I'm in my room after lunch, thinking of Liam as I work on a new sketch of a wedding dress with a halter neckline, when my bedroom door swings open. I know it's Mr. Bordeaux before his shiny black dress shoes come into view on the threshold. Loren warned me he was coming home today, but my heart still seizes in my chest, making breathing difficult as I fling my work aside and scramble to the floor.

He strolls into the room, leaving the door open, and I'm surprised when he takes a seat on the bed, springs squeaking under his weight.

"Loren's reports on your good behavior have been

impressive. I'm glad to know we haven't had anymore incidents."

"Thank you, Mr. Bordeaux."

Pages flutter, and I know he's peering at my doodles. "Loren mentioned you have an interest in fashion design." He flips another page. "You've got talent. If I win the auction for your hand in marriage, we'll have to do something productive with your designs. Would you like that?"

"Yes, Mr. Bordeaux."

"You can speak freely until we leave this room. I think it's time we had a conversation."

A few uncertain moments pass.

"You *do* remember how to speak, don't you? Loren tells me the two of you talk often."

"I'm sorry, Mr. Bordeaux. I'm not sure what to say." It boggles my mind that he thinks I'd *want* to say anything to him.

"Tell me what you think of Loren."

I clench my hands against my thighs then open my fists, once again exposing my palms the way he requires. "He's been kind to me."

"He has a big heart. I have to be careful who I allow near him." He falls silent, and the air thickens with meaning. "He's very important to me, Novalee. I won't hesitate to strike down anyone who threatens his happiness and well-being."

A hard swallow clears my throat. "I won't tell anyone about your relationship."

"You don't like me, do you?"

Is he serious? I'm not even sure how to answer that.

Biting my lip, I force the panic down and try to come up with a diplomatic response, but nothing comes to mind.

"You can be honest, my queen. I won't punish you for it."

"I wish I could like you, Mr. Bordeaux." As the words leave my mouth, I realize they're true. "Disliking someone isn't in my nature, but you haven't given me reason to feel differently." The ensuing disquiet pricks at my nerves, and I gnaw on my lip, worried I revealed too much.

"I appreciate your candidness." There's a melancholy softness to his tone, maybe even a trace of vulnerability. "I can accept your unfavorable opinion of me as long as you have a certain amount of respect and fondness for Loren."

"I do, Mr. Bordeaux."

"Are you attracted to him?"

Loren's large, gray eyes flash through my head. His sensual wide smile. The chemistry isn't there, but I can't deny I find him attractive. "He's gorgeous."

"That's not what I asked."

"I'm not being obtuse, Mr. Bordeaux. I guess I'm not sure what you're asking me."

He rises from the bed and leans down, his warm breath rustling the hair at my ear. "Does he make your pussy wet, my queen?"

A gasp escapes my lips. "N-no."

He settles a hand on my shoulder, fingers grazing the skin left bare from the straps of my sundress. The weather has been warmer these past few days, and with his master's blessing, Loren gave me permission to go outside. Now I wish I'd chosen a dress with sleeves, because I barely tolerate Mr. Bordeaux's touch without flinching.

"Has a man ever made you wet before?" His fingers press into my skin, giving a suggestive squeeze.

"Yes, Mr. Bordeaux."

"Who?"

I hesitate, and his grip tightens, causing me to stumble over Liam's name. "L-Liam...I mean Chancellor Castle."

"Is he the only one?"

All I manage is a shake of my head, vocal cords frozen with shame.

"Who else, Novalee?"

"Sebastian," I choke out.

"Hmm." Removing his touch, he returns to his full height and wanders to my closet. "Am I wrong in assuming this attraction to our resident artist bothers you?"

"No, Mr. Bordeaux. You're not wrong."

"That's interesting," he says, hangers sliding on the rod as he rummages through my meager wardrobe. "And unfortunate for you."

I wait for him to continue, hoping he'll elaborate, but too many moments pass without a hint of what he meant by that comment. I peek at him from under my lashes as he pulls out a blush pink dress that flows to the ankles. It's one of my favorites, the fabric light and soft with thin spaghetti straps that leave my shoulders bare. From the corner of my eye, I watch him drape the garment across my bed.

"Take a shower. Wax and shave and do whatever else you ladies do to make yourselves irresistible." He strides to the door but halts on the threshold. "And don't wear any undergarments. I'll see you in the great room in an hour."

10

The likeness of Evangeline Castle seems to follow me down the hall on the first floor as I walk behind Mr. Bordeaux, my hands clasped at the small of my back. Her portrait is reminiscent of a living entity, the shape of her full lips conveying a secret, the tilt of her stubborn chin urging me to stand my ground, the slits of her knowing eyes taunting me with her own downfall.

Don't fall for the lion, a phantom voice whispers through my mind.

The hairs on the back of my neck stand on end, because Mr. Bordeaux leads me down another hallway, and I suspect he's headed toward Sebastian's studio. Another turn, and we enter through a door, confirming my suspicion.

I'm in the lion's den, and not even the warning from Evangeline's ghost can keep me away.

Mr. Bordeaux comes to a stop, and I sink to my knees as he shoots a glance over his shoulder. Tentatively, I raise my hand.

"Yes, my queen?"

"May I have permission to speak, Mr. Bordeaux?"

"You may."

"Why are we in Sebastian's studio?"

"You've been here before?"

"Yes. Once."

"I have him on retainer. He's going to paint your portrait."

Muffling a gasp, I swallow the burning questions threatening to sprout from my mouth.

Is Sebastian going to paint one of his infamous portraits?

The kind that involve jewels and little else?

Will he be allowed to touch me?

My teeth clamp down on my tongue, slaying the temptation. But God, this rule of not speaking is killing me.

We're alone in Sebastian's studio until the door opens several minutes later, hinges almost silent except for the hyper-tuned state of my ears, and a thrill ignites in my veins. There's no denying I'm excited to see him.

"You were supposed to be here ten minutes ago," Mr. Bordeaux says. From my peripheral, I spy him glancing at the expensive watch on his wrist. "And now I'm late for a conference call."

Footsteps cease moving behind me. Fighting the urge to turn and steal a glance, I focus on the rustic hardwood floor.

"I got held up."

"You get held up a lot, Sebastian."

"Find another artist if it bothers you."

Silence, and then Mr. Bordeaux huffs. "I would if you weren't the best for the job."

"The best will cost you."

"Your fee is already extortion."

"I don't want your money this time."

Mr. Bordeaux gives him an impatient sigh. "What do you want, Sebastian?" My keeper sounds bored as he moves out of sight, and another set of shoes—these the opposite of expensive Italian leather—come into view. I sense the lion's gaze on me as I study his black and white sneakers.

"I want permission to touch her."

Mr. Bordeaux's humorless laugh fills the studio. "Always thinking with your dick."

"It's the best part of me."

"The answer is no."

"Then you'll have to find yourself another artist."

"I don't want another goddamn artist."

I hold my breath, shocked by the slip of Mr. Bordeaux's tongue in front of Sebastian.

"That's my price. Take it or leave it."

Tension steals the next few seconds, and I envision the scowl on Mr. Bordeaux's face because he's not the type to concede. "Fine, you can take your payment from her flesh, but she's not allowed to orgasm."

"You spoil all the fun, Heath."

"Your cock isn't on lockdown, so I'm sure you'll enjoy yourself plenty."

Sebastian laughs. "I'm sure I will."

My heartbeat ratchets with a mixture of fear and lustful excitement.

"You've got three hours. If she's not back in her quarters

by then, she loses a diamond. Same if she comes." More footsteps, and then the finality of a door closing signals Mr. Bordeaux's exit, followed by an inescapable silence that's only amplified by his absence.

Sebastian finally breaks from his statuesque pose, and those black and white sneakers come closer. "I see Heath has worked his usual charm on you."

"How so?"

He bends, lifting my chin with two warm fingers, and the instant our eyes meet, my lips part on a soundless gasp. "The girl I met six years ago wasn't so lifeless, even on her knees."

"Maybe the girl you met six years ago is gone." I tuck my lip between my teeth as memories of the last few weeks flicker through my mind, beginning with the dungeon.

The cold, isolating space, and the endless burn in my knees as I waited for Pax and Mr. Bordeaux to release me from purgatory. The endless loop of insanity as I prayed for hell to spit me back into a semblance of normalcy. But hell only returned me to the stoic, watchful eye of Heath Bordeaux, and that hasn't been much of an improvement.

Sebastian studies me, the brilliance of his azure gaze touching on every inch of my face until I'm flushed with heat.

"I'm not buying it." A slow, cruel smile curves his lips. "Just last month you showed me a taste of that fire on the examination table. That spitfire of a princess is still in there somewhere."

"*Queen*," I say through gritted teeth.

Letting go of me, he raises an amused brow. "I rest my case." He turns and tugs at the back of his T-shirt, yanking it over his tousled blond hair, and I can't help but admire his backside. All of that smooth skin stretched over hard muscle shoots a bolt of desire between my legs. I don't know what it is about Sebastian, but I lose my head whenever he's near.

"You need to take your clothes off for this." He stalks out of sight then returns with a black jewelry case.

"What's that?" I ask, rising to my feet and nodding at the sleek box in his hands.

"It's the Heart of the Queen. Heath finally got his greedy hands on it. I don't know how, but he did." He cracks open the lid. "And he wants me to paint you wearing it." His eyes flick up to meet mine. "Time's ticking. Lose the clothes."

I cross my arms, suddenly unhindered by the training Mr. Bordeaux instilled in me over the last three weeks. "Do you need me naked for the portrait, or for your *payment*?" The word bleeds from my lips, drenched in feigned disgust.

"Both." His grin is rakish, unguarded, and downright sexy. "And since I've only got three hours with you, how about we speed things up?"

He removes the necklace from the box then drapes it around my neck. The teardrop-shaped diamond is a deep scarlet, and the weight of it hangs between my cleavage. I'm gaping at the stone in a state of awe, all too aware that Liam sold this priceless family heirloom because of me, when Sebastian slips a spaghetti strap over my shoulder. He does the same to the other side, followed by a determined tug to the bodice, and the dress falls to the floor.

"No undergarments," he says, voice deepening to an

appreciative rasp as his gaze roams my bare skin. "You came prepared."

"Mr. Bordeaux instructed me not to wear any." The words come out shaky, and I can't bring myself to meet his blue eyes when he looks at me like that.

As if he's starved for the taste of me.

"Let's get something straight," he says, tilting my chin up, "*Mr. Bordeaux* doesn't exist for the next three hours."

"He doesn't?" I breathe, my lips parting because there's that *look* again.

The one that tells me he feels this weird pull between us as much as I do. It's strong and a bit terrifying.

Electrifying.

Liam Castle made me experience things I didn't know I could feel—the highs and lows, the delirious adrenaline rush of several of my *firsts*.

First kiss.

First taste of a man.

First orgasm.

But Sebastian makes me afraid to feel anything at all, because the gamut of emotions he inspires are dangerously intense. This unexplainable connection is nothing but mayhem to my sanity.

"No, Heath Bordeaux doesn't exist in this room. It's just you and me, princess...and the license he gave me to touch you." His smirk should cool the fire heating my veins, but all his cocky confidence seems to do is deliver a direct hit straight to my core.

I shouldn't crave his touch after the way he's treated me, but God help me...

I do.

"I thought you didn't like me." The vulnerability in that admission leaves me exposed before him, my state of undress notwithstanding.

"I *don't* like you."

His confirmation hurts more than it should. More than I'm comfortable with. I search his sea-blue eyes, hoping to uncover a reason—something logical and tangible to explain his dislike—but all I find is reluctant lust.

My brows furrow. "You don't like me...but you want me?"

"God, yes." He steps forward, his impressive bare chest sending me back a few inches, out of the puddle of my dress. "I absolutely want you."

"Why?"

"I don't fucking know. Call it a curse." Another step forward, and his head tilts, eyes narrowed in scrutiny. "Maybe it's the golden silk of your hair and how it makes you seem so young and innocent, or the way you always smell like fruit and flowers." Dipping his head, he runs his nose along my cheekbone. "Some exotic scent that stays with me long after you're gone."

I'm dizzy, my brain spiraling toward the ground, and I've never been more grateful for the perfume I had bottled and sent from home. "It's plumeria."

"It's sexy as hell." He aims his attention on my lips. "But if the smell of you doesn't kill me, the shape of your mouth will, especially all the things it was designed to do."

"What kinds of things?" I dart my tongue along my lower lip, and his pupils dilate.

"Feasting on quivering skin, uttering dirty nothings." He

drags his thumb over my trembling lips. "*Sucking*, Novalee. I bet you do it so well you bring a man to his knees."

"But you don't like me," I remind him in a choked whisper.

"Not even a little."

I'd ask why, but I'm not sure I want to know the answer.

"I don't like you, either," I say instead, willing a smidgeon of truth into the harsh line of my jaw. Willing him to believe the lie...willing the lie to morph into irrefutable truth.

"Glad to hear it, because that makes what I'm about to do much easier." He presses forward until the backs of my legs hit the velvet cushion of a lounge chair. "Sit."

"Wait," I protest. Just because I'm unequivocally attracted to him doesn't mean I'm ready to spread out before him, exposed and vulnerable. It was hard enough doing it the first time, when I was only naked from the waist down, and we had the rest of the Brotherhood surrounding us, not to mention the cold and sterile setting of an examination room as a backdrop. That day, the scorn on his face left no doubt of his feelings toward me.

Now there's something else in his expression. A hunger, a need, a softness that wasn't there before. Maybe even an openness.

And the setting is too cozy and inviting with an undertone of sexual awareness...and we're alone with no distractions on the horizon for the next three hours.

"Novalee, sit your ass down." His voice comes out thick as if he wants to say more but doesn't. "I'm not gonna hurt you."

I hesitate—a deceptive protest—but his irritable

patience wins out. I lower into the chair, limbs tight and awkward as I palm my breasts and press my thighs together, rendered more defenseless than I can stand.

Propping himself up with one hand on the back of the lounge, he leans over and adjusts the necklace until it nestles in the valley of my cleavage. Then, bottom lip tucked between his teeth, he arranges my arms over my head before inching my legs apart to expose my most intimate place.

The one that's inflamed with liquid heat from the press of his fingers on my thighs.

"I saw the portraits you did for him. This isn't how the women posed."

"You're different."

I'm holding my breath, heart diving into a free fall as he sifts my hair between his fingers. The strands slip through his loose grip like fine silk, and he seems mesmerized, further wrecking my shield against this man.

"Why am I different?"

"I never wanted the other models." He arranges the locks over my breasts, and a devious part of me rejoices at the hard-on he's got from fondling my hair.

I'm tempted to grow it to my feet now.

Pushing off the lounge, he strides across the room to where his canvas awaits. As he sets up his supplies and moves a stool in front the easel, I will my cheeks to cool. But I don't harbor such power. It's all I can do to keep my thighs open, because if I close them, and he touches me again, I might beg him for more.

"Stop squirming. I know your pussy's hot and wet, but I need you to stay still for this."

God, I must be a thousand shades of embarrassed. His cruel smirk tells me it's true. Forcing my muscles to relax, I settle in for the next hour as his brush strokes the canvas.

"I've never painted a woman so aroused before." He shoots me a sexy, amused smile.

"Were your previous subjects zombies?" The retort escapes before I can stop it.

His grin widens. "They were as hot-blooded as you, princess. Just not as innocent."

I despise how the nickname has grown on me. He's the only one who calls me that. And he's the only one, besides Liam, who makes me want to shed my innocence. A sharp pang radiates through my chest, because my intense attraction to Sebastian feels like a betrayal to Liam.

At the end of the first hour, he shifts in front of his work. "You're fucking gorgeous. I can't wait for you to see it."

I sit forward, but he gives a stern shake of his head. "I didn't say you could move."

"I want to see it."

"You will, *after*." Abandoning the paintbrush, he saunters in my direction.

"It's time for your payment, then?" I arch a challenging brow, but I'm shaking on the inside. The closer his purposeful steps bring him, the quicker my composure crumbles.

"Something like that." He halts between my legs, rough denim grazing my inner thighs, and my toes curl as his gaze travels the length of my body. "You heard the man. No orgasms."

I bite back a whimper, fighting to keep my thighs from pressing against his legs. "He's evil."

Sebastian laughs. "To you, maybe." Putting one hand on the back of the lounge, he leans over until we're face to face. "But I'm going to enjoy this." Slowly, he dips his fingers between my legs, and I swallow a moan.

I'm putty in his hands.

"It's a shame I'll have to deprive this wet pussy." He adds a teasing caress to my clit.

My hips jerk, seeking a firmer touch. "I-I need—"

"You need to sit still and take it," he interrupts. "I have two hours left to play with you, and you're not allowed to come." To add insult to injury, he plunges a finger into my tight opening, and there's no hiding a moan this time.

"You don't have to tell him."

His smile is downright smug. "Oh, I'll tell him."

"Why are you doing this?"

"Because leaving you on the edge gets me hot."

I impale myself on his finger, only easing up when it starts to pinch, and he picks up the rhythm, that digit sliding in and out of me until I'm moaning for more. "Sebastian, please."

"My name, your lips...pure fucking heaven, princess."

I say his name again, and he *growls* at me.

Like an animal.

An alpha of the pack catching a whiff of his mate.

"If you don't tell me to stop, I'll let him know how drenched and needy you are right before you come. I'll describe the flush of your cheeks, and how tight your cunt feels around my fingers, clenching with each...forbidden... wave." He leans forward, his bright blue eyes locking onto mine, lips parted, breath shuddering against my mouth. "He'll take away one of your precious diamonds."

"Stop," I gasp, exerting pure willpower to stall my hips.

"Are you sure?" His touch slows, fingers teasing my wet slit, and I groan my frustration.

The only thing I'm sure of is that I want him to keep going.

"No," I say instead, suffering from a case of indecision.

"Beg me to stop playing with your pussy, and I will."

"I don't want you to stop!" I squeeze my eyes shut, caught in a mental trap. "Please...I need you."

"You can have me, princess, but not without consequences."

He's too smug, over-the-top cocky, and ridiculously sexy.

And I'm too powerless in this fight, the battle lost before he even touched me. But I'm not a quitter, so I do the only thing I can.

I go on the offense.

"Let me see you," I say, reaching for the button of his ripped jeans. His eyes darken, and my heart dances in triumph. Glory is on the horizon, and it's *mine*. I lick my lips, drunk off the sudden advantage I taste on my tongue.

Power is the lust in his eyes.

And the throbbing member in his pants is my weapon.

This is war.

He swats my hands away, pulls down his zipper, and then he's straddling my thighs as his massive erection stands between us.

"So what'll it be? Am I fucking that tempting mouth, or do I have to settle for your fists?" He dips his head, lips brushing my ear. "Or I could take your virgin ass."

"How do you know I haven't already...done that?"

"Liam doesn't have the balls to take you like that." His teeth clamp onto my earlobe, and he gives a playful tug. "And we both know Heath hasn't laid a finger on you. So, that leaves a blow job, or a hand job...unless you *want* the third option? Either way, you're getting the job done."

"H-hand job," I say, tripping over the words.

He pushes upright again and yanks my hands between us, and my fingers wrap around hard, smooth flesh. Our gazes lock as his hands guide mine on his shaft, up and down in tight, long strokes.

"Fuck, that feels good."

He's huge, spanning the stack of my fists and then some, and I'm glued to the sight of his tip popping through the top of our joined hands. A drop of moisture leaks from the crown. He increases the tempo, pumping in quick, jerky motions, then frantically shoves my hair out of the way, ordering me to keep up the pace.

"I'm gonna come so fucking hard all over those tits."

My body responds to the gravelly sound of his voice, the rapid soughing of his breaths, and I feel my nipples tighten, begging for him to follow through on his promise. He throws his head back with a groan, and seconds later, his warm, thick release spurts onto my chest.

Silence descends in the moments that follow. Sebastian grips the back of the lounge, eyes shuttered as he catches his breath.

He's beautiful in the aftermath.

As if he heard the unspoken thought, he lifts his lids, and our gazes collide. I've never wanted him as much as I do now, trapped beneath his body, and drenched between the thighs as his cum bathes my chest.

Almost reverently, he kneads my breasts, smearing his release all over the jewel nestled between them. "We tainted his precious diamond." He gives my nipples a hard pinch. "My cum is all over his property."

The double meaning isn't lost on me.

Because that's all I am to someone like Heath Bordeaux. A possession, a thing to stow away with the rest of his treasures.

And to Sebastian, I'm just a plaything, easily taunted by his cruelty.

Masking the hurt rising inside me, I push against his chest. "You got your payment. Now I want to see my painting."

He stands, zips up his pants, then helps me to my feet. "Turned out uncannily accurate, if you ask me."

I'm not sure what he means until I'm standing in front of his masterpiece, blinking in astonishment at the familiar face staring back.

Her skin flushed and lips dewy.

Textured shadows obscuring her more intimate areas, offering a sense of modest seduction.

But those expressive brown eyes impart every thought and emotion she doesn't want the world to see.

That's me on that canvas...and I can't believe it.

"She's beautiful," I whisper, awestruck at how he captured me. At how he *sees* me.

He lingers behind me, heat penetrating my backside, and curls his fingers around my shoulders. "Because you are, Novalee."

The girl in the painting is tastefully positioned, sexily aroused, and she gazes at her audience with aching want in her bedroom eyes.

It's a picture that spells desire.

Testifies to her desperation.

And she's directing every bit of her longing at the artist.

If Liam ever sets eyes on this painting, he'll see it too.

11

Keeping my promise to Liam has never been so difficult. In the days since Sebastian painted my portrait, I've had to fight myself too many times to count. Because I've never ached to touch myself the way I do now, and I don't want to let Liam down by breaking the promise I made to him.

So when I meet him for our second chess game, I'm certain shame lingers in my eyes. So does this incessant ache between my legs, reignited by his long kiss upon greeting me.

"You're quiet today." He slides his bishop across the board. "Is everything okay?"

Moving a pawn, I capture one of his, but I find no joy in the conquest. Because I can't lie to him—we established that dynamic early in our relationship.

But God, I don't want to hurt him.

"What's wrong, Novalee?" A frown plays at the corners of his lips.

I settle back in my chair and hold his gaze. "Sebastian painted my portrait last week."

He's quiet for several moments. "You wore the diamond."

It's more of a statement, but I nod anyway.

"I knew it was a possibility when I sold the necklace to Heath." He shifts in his chair. "What's bothering you about it, my sweet girl?"

"I don't want to hurt you." The admission splashes a cold aura over the room.

"Then be honest with me."

"Sebastian didn't want money for the portrait," I say, skirting the issue.

"Of course he didn't." Certainty hardens his tone. "He wanted to touch you."

Shame clogs my throat, and everything I don't say darkens his eyes.

"What did he get in exchange for his services?"

"I already told you. He touched—"

"I want details," he cuts in.

My heartbeat thunders behind my breastbone, and no matter how hard I try, I can't pull in a full breath. "I'm not giving you details."

He watches me, tense with jealousy, his chin resting on his clenched hand. "Did you come?"

"I wasn't allowed to."

"But you wanted to, didn't you?"

"Yes," I admit through gritted teeth, hating the undeniable anger that shadows his gorgeous face. "And now I can't stop thinking about touching myself."

His nostrils flare in surprise. "You kept your promise?"

"It hasn't been easy."

"It's not supposed to be easy, Novalee." He leans forward, chess game abandoned on the table between us. "It's supposed to teach you obedience, patience, and control."

"It's teaching me resentment."

"I disagree. Abstaining is teaching you that your pussy belongs to me, even when eleven other men think they can claim it."

The fervor in his tone shoots straight between my thighs, and I press them together, growing hotter and wetter by the second. The more we verbally spar, the more I want to push my hand into my panties.

"Please," I whisper, the plea a breathless whine. "Let me touch myself."

"No."

"I need the release, Liam. I'm begging you."

"If I give you permission, will you think of him when you bring yourself to orgasm?"

The memory of Sebastian astride my thighs, shirtless and shameless, his cock standing proud between us, almost makes me whimper.

"I...I-I don't know." My answer doesn't earn me any points with him.

"And if I forbid you, will you still keep your promise?"

Futile tears burn my eyes. "Yes."

Resting his hands between his knees, he dips his head. "So you're loyal to me, but you burn for him."

"It's not that simple, Liam." A drop of heartache splashes onto my cheekbone. "You're not being fair."

With a sigh, he stands and rounds the table. "Nothing

about this situation is simple or fair, my sweet girl." He thumbs away the teardrop on my skin. "You have my heart, but you don't have my permission."

"Please," I beg again, blinking two more tears down my cheeks.

He bends long enough to press his lips to mine. "So long as Sebastian is the reason for the ache between your legs, the answer is no."

"It's *my* body," I say, righteous defiance boiling to the surface. "You can't stop me."

Instead of angering him, my mock rebellion evokes a sorrowful slant to his kissable lips. "You're right, I can't stop you, but your loyalty to me will."

He says nothing more as he turns toward the door of the library, cutting our session short. It shuts upon his exit with an anticlimactic click, and the last of my composure shatters. I sob into my hands, chest splintering from the onslaught of his hurt and disappointment.

Because I'm inconsolable in my grief, and at a loss to do anything about it.

12

I feign a stomach bug for the next few days as explanation for my heartbroken, lifeless state of mind since things blew up between Liam and me.

But today my mood shifts as soon as the sun rises, because it's my last day in the House of Taurus.

It also happens to be my keeper's birthday.

Loren and I prepare a celebratory dinner featuring Mr. Bordeaux's favorite dishes of creamy pesto shrimp and grilled zucchini.

My keeper's mood is abnormally pleasant, and I'm a little perplexed by his willingness to be a decent human being tonight, going so far as to let me sit at the table and speak. He even gave us free rein on choosing the menu for the evening.

I'm in the kitchen loading the dishwasher when I sense his presence behind me. Turning to face him, I lower to my haunches and strike the pose.

"Did Loren tell you today is his birthday, too?"

"No, Mr. Bordeaux. He didn't."

"I'm not surprised." He wanders to the dishwasher, and much to my astonishment, stacks the last two dessert bowls on the top rack. "He always puts the focus on me, even though this is his day too."

That's because Loren is selfless. Mr. Bordeaux could learn a thing or two from his manservant.

"This year, I have something special in mind for him." Switching on the dishwasher, he trains his attention on me. "And you're going to help me."

"Whatever you need, Mr. Bordeaux."

"You mean that, don't you?" His fingers lift my chin, and it takes every ounce of willpower not to catch his gaze and try to find a reason for his oddly softened tone.

"Yes, Mr. Bordeaux."

"I know your first instinct is to tell me what I want to hear, but I believe I can trust you." His touch strengthens to a strong, unmovable grip on my jaw. "Look at me, Novalee."

Inch by inch, I draw my gaze along the slope of his shoulder, the evening stubble on his jawline, the thin point of his nose, and finally…I meet his hazel eyes.

"Despite your occasional stumble, you've proven your obedience and, dare I say, loyalty." He tilts his head. "I know you have a soft spot for Loren."

"He's been very kind to me."

"Where I have not."

I don't answer because confirming his assessment won't do either of us any good.

"You might not like what I have in mind tonight, but I expect you to cooperate for Loren's sake."

"I understand, Mr. Bordeaux."

He rubs his thumb across my lip. "Tonight, you will address Loren as your master. If you fail to do so, you will lose a diamond, and I'll be forced to schedule your punishment with Pax." A beat goes by, in which he gives me a pointed look. "Am I correct in assuming you don't want such a visit to the dungeon hanging over your head as you move on to the House of Gemini tomorrow?"

"You're correct, Mr. Bordeaux. That's not what I want."

"Then we understand each other. Follow me." He ushers me out of the kitchen, through the great room, and into his private quarters, and the sight beyond the double doors doesn't fully register until I stall three feet inside my keeper's bedroom. My breath stalls in my lungs.

Loren is kneeling.

In *the* pose.

And he's completely naked.

The doors shut behind me, and Mr. Bordeaux gestures to a reclining lounge next to the king-sized bed. "Take a seat," he tells me, nodding toward the chair.

I obey, but the unmoving sight of Loren tugs at my attention. He's kneeling to the right of me, where Mr. Bordeaux approaches him with his unhurried, confident gait.

"Go ahead and stand," he orders, voice too husky to be demanding.

Loren rises to his feet. He's a couple inches shy of his master's height, but no less imposing in his naked beauty.

Before I came to the island, I would have fallen over in mortification at witnessing such a display of unabashed nudity, but the men living inside the circular walls of the

Zodiac Estate have thoroughly corrupted me in the last two months.

"Stand in front of Novalee. Show her what a gorgeous cock you have."

There's a hint of shyness in Loren's mannerisms as he halts before me, hands at his back. His hard-on confronts me at eye-level, despite the reclined position of my body.

"You're her master tonight, my love. She answers to you." Mr. Bordeaux reaches for Loren's erection from behind, and his fingers wrap around the base. "She's my gift to you."

"You've already given me so much, Master Bordeaux. A gift isn't necessary."

"Nothing is necessary, but I want to give this to you. You deserve a warm, wet place for this beautiful cock to go." His strokes quicken, and Loren shudders. "You want to come, don't you, my love?"

"Yes," he hisses, jerking into his master's fist.

"Then choose. Do you want to use her mouth, or her ass?"

Loren's heavy-lidded gaze meets mine, and I silently plead for the first option, my expression stricken at the thought of option two.

"She has a beautiful mouth, Master Bordeaux."

"Yes, she does. She's beautiful through and through. Would you like to see her without clothing?"

"Y-yes."

"Then command her. You *are* her master tonight. She knows not to disobey you."

Loren licks his lips, the dart of his tongue more nervous than seductive. "I want you to remove your dress," he tells me, lacking the hard-edged tone of his master.

I pull at the hem and work the dress up my torso and over my head, then I shimmy out of my panties, ass scooting on the soft leather cushion. My nipples pebble in the mild temperature of the room, and Loren's gaze latches onto them. With a deep-throated groan, he pushes into his master's hand.

Mr. Bordeaux squeezes the tip, making Loren wince.

"I know she's sexy, but you don't get to come until I say you do." Mr. Bordeaux's zipper sounds, along with other movements that go unseen, and then he grips Loren's hips, and by the way they both jerk, I know Mr. Bordeaux is claiming his ass. Teeth clenched, Loren hisses in a breath at the intrusion.

Muscular thighs slap against skin, chests heave, and cocks thrust—Loren's into Mr. Bordeaux's fist as his master seeks pleasure from behind.

"I need more," Loren rasps, grunting a rhythmic song of agony laced with pleasure. Anytime he gets close to climaxing, Mr. Bordeaux squeezes the tip of his shaft.

That's when I realize he's using the maneuver to keep him from reaching orgasm.

"Do you want inside her mouth?"

"Yes, Master Bordeaux," he groans.

"Then make her open for you." The two tilt forward, and Loren holds onto the back of the lounge, his arms extended, muscles bulging from exertion as he thrusts the tip toward my lips.

"Do you want this?" Loren asks, dipping his head and searching my face.

I'm intrigued, and a little turned on watching them, but the honest answer is *no*, and I'm certain that isn't what he's hoping to hear.

"Y-yes...Master."

I can do this for him, and I try to tell him so by holding his gaze as I part my lips.

Loren only hesitates a second before pushing inside. "Ah, God, Novalee."

He's heavy on my tongue, a mixture of salt and his own unique essence, and I work him the best I can, part of me wanting to give him pleasure.

The bigger part of me wants this to be over.

The three of us settle into a steady tempo, connected by sex and lust and submissive roles. Mr. Bordeaux pounds into Loren, his thrusts violent enough to pummel the cock in my mouth to the back of my throat.

I grab the cushion beneath me, fingers digging into leather, and hold on for all I'm worth. That's all I *can* do—remain still, mouth spread wide as Loren rides my face. He's so deep that the circle of Mr. Bordeaux's fist pushes against my lips, gripping Loren at the base.

Every few minutes, he yanks Loren from my mouth and stops his orgasm with firm pressure to the head.

"Let me come, Master Bordeaux. Please."

"Aren't you enjoying her mouth?"

"Yes. Feels so good." Loren shutters his eyes in frustration.

"When I come, you come." Mr. Bordeaux gives a dark chuckle. "You should feel privileged, my love. Our beautiful queen doesn't get to come at all."

The reminder is a smack to the face, a splash of ice

water on the sweat-inducing haze of depravity in the room. My mind steamrolls over the memory of my argument with Liam a few days ago, then slams into the brick wall of Sebastian's taunting denial.

It seems every man in this tower wants to put my orgasms on lockdown.

Loren thrusts into my mouth again, and then Mr. Bordeaux grunts, both hands gouging Loren's hips as he groans a series of unintelligible cries. He empties into his lover, and that sends Loren over the edge. His release is a fountain of completion, intense and prolonged from his master's game of stopping and starting. I choke and cough as his climax hits the back of my throat, but afterward...

Loren smiles down at me, skin bathed in sweat, gray eyes brimming with gratitude, and I can't find an iota in me that regrets being part of his pleasure.

13

Perhaps last night was an appropriate send-off, a depraved bon voyage for a virgin queen in metaphorical chains. Or maybe I've been used and degraded to the point where the after-dinner affair inside that bedroom seems normal.

Either way, I'm excited to put Mr. Bordeaux and his esoteric tastes behind me. I spend my last moments under his rule saying goodbye to Loren, since his master is absent when the clock strikes the noon hour. Loren thanks me for a night he'll never forget, and then he wishes me luck.

Unlike last month, I'm alone, nervous energy infusing my steps as I approach the library. The door stands open—an unspoken invite to breach the threshold and give myself over to a new set of expectations, a new set of rules, a new man.

I've barely stepped inside the library when Faye wraps her arms around me. "I'm so glad to see you." She veers back and studies my face. "How are you?"

"I'm okay." I give her a squeeze before we break apart.

"Where's Elise?" I search the room, my gaze touching on the dark-haired man standing to the right of us, but my lady is notably absent. "Is she okay?"

Because she'd be here if she were.

"She's fine." Faye averts her attention to the floor.

"Faye, what's wrong?" A cold fist of worry clenches my gut.

"She's been...ill for the past few days, but she's okay."

She's not telling me everything. On the cusp of panic, I glance at Landon for an explanation.

"Elise is okay." He closes the distance and takes me by the arm, and I flinch from his touch.

It's becoming an ingrained reflex when stumbling blindly into new territory. "I-I'm sorry." Out of habit, I almost kneel at his feet.

"You're not in Heath's house anymore," he reminds me with a gentle tug on my arm. "Come sit down."

I follow him to the same grouping of chairs Liam and I used during our chess games, and we settle across from each other. Faye takes a chair to my left.

"She's really okay?" I direct the question at Landon.

"She will be." He reaches for a mauve journal sitting on the table between us, and something about it niggles at me to pay attention, but I'm too worried about the well-being of my lady.

"What happened?"

"There was an incident, but I'm handling it."

"What kind of *incident*?" The vague run-around I'm getting from both Landon and Faye has me on the edge of crazy.

Faye clears her throat. "She wants to tell you herself."

I move to rise, and Landon stays me with a raised hand. "She's not here, my queen."

"Where is she?" I shout, hands fisted against the arms of my seat.

"She's returning to Zodiac Island this evening and will tell you everything then." Landon leans forward, expression drawn in tension. It's a foreign look on him, because he's normally open and carefree, eyes glinting like emeralds.

Now those eyes are jaded, shrouded in concern over whatever information he's withholding in my lady's honor.

"You really won't tell me anything?"

"Elise asked me not to." Clearing his throat, he holds out the journal. "But we need to discuss this."

The book is bound in leather, its ribbon keeping the jacket closed to shut out prying eyes. I've seen many of its kind because my mother had a whole collection.

"What about it?" I take the journal from Landon, and as soon as my thumb glides over the front cover and the handwritten initials there, a memory explodes in my mind. A shocked breath catches in my throat, rendering speech impossible, yet I force the question out anyway.

"Where did you get this?"

Landon and Faye exchange a heavy glance.

"It belonged to your mother," he says, the confirmation pinning me to the chair in a state of frozen disbelief. "We have a lot to talk about, my queen."

GEMINI

BOOK THREE

1

MAY 21ST

We have a lot to talk about, my queen. As Landon's words reverberate through my head, I trace the familiar inscribed letters on the journal. My fingers move in a hypnotic way as the breath stalls in my lungs. Because it's one of my mother's diaries, and even if he hadn't told me it belonged to her, I'd recognize it by those initials written in elegant calligraphy.

"How did you get this?" My voice is sharp and brazen—the kind of tone that would earn me a session in the dungeon if I were still under the rule of Heath Bordeaux.

Landon glances at my lady. "Faye, will you give us a few minutes?" With a cooperative nod, she gets up to leave, and the fact that she's not fighting him surprises me as much as the familiar way in which he addressed her.

After the door shuts upon her exit, he leans forward, hands clasped between his knees. "What do you know about your mother's journals?"

An image of leather spines, sorted by color, comes to mind—a neat row kept dust-free on an oak shelf in her writing room. After she died, my uncle turned the space into storage.

"She had a collection. She was always writing between the pages. After the crash..." With a hard swallow, I pause. "My uncle boxed them up, but Faye's mother gave them to me on my sixteenth birthday."

"Did you read them?"

I shift, crossing my left ankle over my right. My mother was a romantic at heart, right until the day she died at my father's side on that plane. She wrote everything from poems to artistic descriptions of the mundane hours that made up her days. Thinking of those journals renews my sorrow, and my eyes burn with it. No matter how much time passes, grief festers in my soul, a permanent scar waiting for the right trigger to peel away the scabs and uncover the hurt as if it burrowed there yesterday.

"I read every word she ever wrote."

He points to the diary in my hands. "You didn't read that one."

"How can you be certain?"

"You'd know the truth if you had."

"The truth?"

Rising to his feet, Landon wanders to the windows. Unlike last month, when the sun shone on the imposing form of Mr. Bordeaux, turning his midnight hair a bluish silver, cloud cover greets Landon on the other side of that glass. His faded black jeans and olive button-down shirt complement the tumultuous slate sky. Maybe it's a fitting backdrop for whatever "truth" the man from the House of Gemini is about to impart.

A few seconds slip by before he turns to face me. "I

don't know how else to say this, so I'm just going to put it out there. Your mother and my father had an affair nineteen years ago."

His "truth" blasts through my consciousness, as abrupt and loud as a gunshot, and my heart beats with an irregular rhythm. I work my jaw, mouth gaping and shutting before falling open again. "I don't believe you."

My parents loved each other. They were happy and faithful and...and my mother wouldn't have done this.

Not *nineteen* years ago.

"It's the truth, Novalee."

The conviction in his voice shoots dread into my gut. "There must be some kind of mistake," I say, smoothing my thumb over my mother's initials on the cover, as if the action will smooth the ripples of turmoil bubbling inside me.

"There's no mistake." He nods at the leather-bound journal I'm clutching like a lifeline. "She wrote about it in detail."

I toss the diary on the table as if it burned me. "Then it's a forgery!"

"It's not a forgery." Reclaiming his seat, he softens his tone, and his emerald eyes bore into me, willing me to believe him. "Faye gave it to me when you arrived on the island. Her mother kept the journal hidden after your parents died."

My eyes widen. "How long has Faye known about this?"

"As far as I'm aware, just a few months."

Betrayal lingers on my tongue like a bitter pill I don't want to swallow. "How could she not tell me?" The question is rhetorical, laden with stunned disbelief.

Landon answers anyway. "Her mother swore her to secrecy."

"That's no excuse! She's my lady...my best friend since childhood. This doesn't make any sense." I narrow my eyes. "Why would she give the journal to you?"

"To ensure I don't bid in the auction."

I can't breathe, can't think...I don't *want* to think. Because thinking means analyzing his explanation, rolling it around in my mind and coming to heartbreaking facts based on inference. It means admitting, even to myself, that what he's saying might be true. The thought torpedoes through my mind, and I think back to the last two months.

Landon and his kind, secretive eyes.

The way he pushed back against Heath on my behalf at last month's dinner.

And how he gave me an "out" at the medical examination and was the first to leave when given the choice.

How he didn't touch me...*at all*.

"Just say it," I demand, voice tremoring with devastation.

"You're my sister."

I shake my head...denying, denying, denying.

"But I have the Van Buren eyes, and..." As I bite my lip, a tear escapes my lashes.

"Biologically, you're the daughter of Franklin Astor." Glancing down at his joined hands, Landon pauses. "You have my father's smile...not that you've had reason to smile since arriving on the island."

The heaviness of his words, the quiet sadness in them, float between us for several moments, and the raging hurt in my soul ebbs a little. My gaze lands on the abandoned journal sitting between us. I wipe my cheeks, stowing away the anguish to deal with later when I'm alone.

"Did you know before Faye gave you the diary?"

"My father told me last year."

"Who else knows?"

"No one, other than Faye and her mother." He rakes a hand through his thick, dark hair, disrupting the combed-back strands. "If the truth comes out that you descend from Evangeline Castle..." Landon lets out a quick breath. "The Brotherhood will void the contract. There will be no auction for marriage."

My heart skips a hopeful beat. "You mean I'll be able to leave this place?"

"Where will you go? As the only living relative of King Van Buren, Rowan *is* the rightful heir to the throne of your lands." He falls silent, letting the statement settle between us.

Letting it sink in.

Because if Franklin Astor is my father, then I have no legal claim on my home, other than the precious memories of growing up there. I'm parentless, and until my twenty-first birthday—when I can access my trust fund—I'm penniless.

"I want to go home." I cross my arms, a pure display of defiance because deep down, I know I'm screwed whether I stay or go.

With a sigh, Landon rises and closes the few feet between us. Kneeling in front of me, he takes my hand in his. "Going home isn't an option, my queen."

I yank my hand free. "I'm not your queen. According to what you just told me, I'm *nobody's* queen."

"You *are* a queen, Novalee. For the sake of your nation, no one must find out about our shared bloodline. That's why I'll continue to address you so formally. The auction must go on."

"So you won't allow me to leave?"

He shakes his head. "You're an Astor." Something flashes in his emerald gaze, something I can't define though it's on the edge of my mind, scratching with a hint of clarity. "You belong on Zodiac Island, *not* with Rowan or out in the world on your own."

I nod toward my mother's secret journal. Her Pandora's box. "You might have the power to keep me here, but you can't stop me from revealing the truth myself."

The transformation in Landon's expression has me pressing into the back of the chair, regretting my threat. He leans forward, his face a harsh mask of warning. "You don't want to see the other side of me. For the sake of you and your nation, this is a secret you *will* keep."

"Issuing threats isn't a very brotherly thing to do."

His mouth flattens into a stubborn line. "I'm not the bad guy in this situation, Novalee, but I'll do whatever is necessary to protect you and keep you here where you belong."

I can't help but glare at him because he's treating me the same way every other man in this tower has—like a puppet to be mastered.

"You'd rather see me married to someone like Heath Bordeaux?"

"Heath won't get his hands on you again."

"But he has the means to win the auction."

"He'll have to stick to art and jewels. The auction for your hand isn't one he's going to win."

"You sound certain."

"I am." He stands, and the weight of his stare presses on me. "There's only one man I'll allow to win that auction."

"Who?" A dart of my tongue moistens my dry, nervous lips.

He folds his arms, a flawless statue of confident authority. "Someone I trust with my life. Someone I trust with this secret...someone you've got an eye for." The knowing smirk on his face is a preamble, and he lets it hang.

"*Who?*" I demand again, bracing myself.

"Sebastian."

2

Sebastian, the lion. The man with the most brilliant blue eyes I've ever seen. A man who *hates* me.

And Landon plans to marry me off to him.

Landon Astor...my *brother*.

"Are you going to give me the silent treatment all day?" Faye's voice dips, a moment away from cracking in distress.

Or growling in frustration.

I'm not sure which, and considering all she kept from me, what she's *still* keeping from me—if I count the mystery of what happened to Elise—I can't say I care about Faye's state of mind.

Not when my own is spinning with the revelations Landon dropped on me no more than an hour ago.

"You'll have to talk to me eventually," she tries again.

Ignoring her, I keep my gaze trained on the endless expanse of ocean in the distance. The French doors stand open, allowing the crisp scent of spring to filter into my new quarters in the House of Gemini.

The set of rooms Landon gave me are the most luxurious and spacious I've encountered in this tower. The smell of fresh paint and new upholstery hint that he had the space renovated.

To ensure the rooms are fit for a queen? Or fit for family?

"I wanted to tell you, but my mother swore me to secrecy." Faye fidgets in the bistro-style chair across from me, sandwiches and tea untouched on the table between us. "She thought you'd hear it best from Landon."

Now I do look at her, my eyes narrowed in disbelief. "As opposed to hearing life-altering news from my lady and best friend—someone who's like a sister to me?"

"Landon is a figure of power and authority. She thought you'd believe him over me."

"That's ridiculous and you know it."

"You're right," she concedes, her voice soft with defeat. "She couldn't risk you going public with the truth. That's why she felt the news had to come from Landon."

"So she *wants* me to be passed around like a whore?"

Faye flinches. "She wants what's best for you."

"I find that hard to believe. Regardless of her skewed reasoning, your loyalty should have been to me."

"I'm sorry I betrayed your trust, but I couldn't go against my mother."

"You've never had a problem with rebellion before."

She averts her gaze, guilt flushing her cheeks, and I realize she's still holding something back.

"What's the real reason you kept your mouth shut?"

Hesitation pulls at her ruby-painted lips. "My mother said I could return home if I promised to deliver the journal to Landon."

Her confession is a punch to the gut, and I struggle to breathe, to find the right words to convey the level of devastation and betrayal rushing through me right now.

"Well you kept your promise, so you're free to go." I wave my hand toward the door of my private quarters. "I'm relieving you of your duties as my lady."

Faye's lashes flutter, eyes bright with unchecked emotion. "I don't want to leave like this."

"Just go," I say through gritted teeth.

"Novalee," she pleads.

"As your *queen*, I command you to leave." The order ricochets off the walls before settling between us, as impenetrable as a steel barrier.

Faye bites her lip as she rises, and the tear that slides down her cheek almost breaks through my armor. I harden my heart against the forgiveness tugging at me. Forgiveness will take time; forgetting how she withheld such momentous information will take longer.

It doesn't matter that deep down I know she did it for love—for the chance to return to the home she misses and the one man who has her heart. Right now, I'm incapable of offering understanding, let alone empathy.

In the absence of Faye's guilt-ridden presence, my mother's journal calls to me from the side table where Landon left it. Uncertainty constricts my throat as I pick up the leather-bound book. Before he left Faye and me alone to talk, he asked me to read my mother's words.

Her confession from the grave.

A huge part of me is delaying, because as soon as I read the truth, written in my mother's beautiful penmanship, I'll have no choice but to accept that everything I know about my childhood is a lie. Curling up in the window seat by the fireplace, I open the cover. The first entry is dated almost a year before I was born.

March 8th

It's been a month since I've written. Seems like forever, but at the same time, too little time has passed. I'm not ready for this.

I'll never be ready.

Putting everything into words is a foolish thing to do, but my heart needs to spill this burden. Edwin and I have been trying to conceive for three years, to no avail. The pressure to produce an heir has been a strain on our marriage. Even worse, it's a threat to our country's security.

Rowan is watching our every move, salivating at the idea that we might not produce an heir within the allotted timeframe. The man is a power-hungry narcissist. His vision for the future of our nation doesn't align with Edwin's. He believes a dictatorship is the only way to ensure loyalty from the people, while Edwin rules with compassion and empathy.

Too much is at stake, and that's how I justify what we're about to do.

Because we only have two years left to conceive, and the doctor we saw at the beginning of the year said Edwin is infertile.

I guess I should back up a bit. Our desperate solution presented itself last month at the diplomacy summit. From the moment I laid eyes on Franklin Astor, I knew he was a powerful man. The way he watched me from across the room made me uncomfortable, but there was no denying the way he commanded the space around him.

I'm not sure Edwin noticed the other man's scrutiny, but later that night when Mr. Astor cornered us in the hall, he had my husband's full attention.

Because Franklin Astor, this mysterious and handsome man from a small island up north, couldn't keep his hungry eyes off of me. Then he did the unthinkable.

He offered us a proposition we couldn't ignore—an ungodly amount of money for one night with me.

Of course, we were shocked at first, so Mr. Astor gave us his number and told us to think about it. That's all we did that night, unable to sleep as a disturbing idea took hold in the dead of night, because there was only one thing we needed and it wasn't more money.

The next morning, we countered with our own offer and made a deal.

That day feels like it took place a lifetime ago, but now that we've flown to Zodiac Island in the wee hours of the morning out of a necessity for discretion, our decision is much too real. Dread and self-loathing fill my stomach as I write this, because we're doing this.

And once we do, there's no going back.

The date's entry stops there, and I set aside the journal as I process what my mother wrote. A sense of relief storms through me, because at least she didn't have a secret affair behind my father's back. He was complicit in the affair, an accomplice to the illicitness of it.

They did it for our country.

They did it to produce an heir.

And I wouldn't be here if they hadn't.

With a deep breath, I pick up the journal and turn to the next page.

March 9th

I've done things in my life that have inspired a sense of shame, regardless of whether it was warranted. Nothing will ever compare to the cloak of shame that shrouds me now. I deserve it, and though part of me knows it isn't fair, I deserve the disappointment in Edwin's eyes too.

Because now there's a secret between us, an "incident" we both agreed we wouldn't discuss. Ever.

I'm not allowed to tell him the details of what happened in Franklin Astor's private quarters. The memory of his hands on my breasts, his mouth between my thighs, the fullness of him inside me are secrets I'll carry with me to my grave.

That was the pact Edwin and I made.

We're on our way home now, and the silence between us is heartbreaking. I have faith we'll find a way through this together, after some time has passed.

But what if I didn't conceive?

What if we have to make the decision to go back next month and try again?

The next several entries are a chronicle of how my parents worked through their decision to bring a third person into their bedroom. Though to be accurate, the bedroom belonged to Franklin Astor. For the weeks following that night, resentment and disappointment festered because the gamble didn't produce the results they prayed for. My mother didn't get pregnant.

But I wouldn't be here today if they hadn't gone back and tried again.

Time runs away from me as I become immersed in the pages, shocked to my core as the truth unfolds. My mother spent two more nights with Franklin Astor before she conceived, and in exchange for his contractual agreement to relinquish all parental rights to my parents, my mother agreed to visit his bed once a year until he no longer wished for her to do so.

Reaching the end of the journal, I close it and set it back on the table. The call of seagulls drift into the room, but otherwise it's utterly quiet. I sit, unmoving, fighting tears as I wrap my head around everything I learned today. I don't want to believe it, but my mother's words are indisputable evidence.

Edwin Van Buren was not my biological father.

A soft knock startles me from my stupor, and I lift my head as Liam steps into the sitting room. He closes the distance but stops before coming within touching distance, and I can't ignore the awkwardness between us after the way we left things the last time I saw him, when he forbade me from touching myself.

"Are you okay?" he asks.

"I'm fine." The lie rolls off my tongue without hesitation, and a small ping of regret arrows through my heart. Lying to Liam Castle isn't something I want to do, but I don't have a choice.

With a sigh, he takes a step closer. "You don't seem fine.

Faye didn't, either. She just left the island."

I knew she'd leave, but hearing confirmation hurts more than I thought it would. "She wasn't happy here, so I relieved her of her duties."

"I'm sorry to hear that. I know how close the two of you are."

"I appreciate your use of the present tense." For the first time since discovering her betrayal, a niggle of forgiveness aches in my chest, and I blink, sending a bitter tear down my cheek. Before I know it, they're escaping my eyes like a faucet with a constant drip. "I could use your arms right now. Is that against the rules?"

"Fuck the rules, Novalee." He reaches for me, and I launch into his embrace, sucking in a deep, satisfying breath as his arms tighten around me.

"It's been an emotional day." I tilt my chin up, and he keeps me in check by cradling my cheeks.

"Novalee." My name is a simple plea, because he knows what I want—the haze in his brown eyes deepen as they focus on my lips. "I'm dying to kiss you, trust me on this, but I'd better not push it."

"Does Landon know you're here?"

"Yes. He took Faye to the airstrip. He's also picking up Elise." He searches my face, his thumbs brushing the sensitive spots under my ears. "I wasn't aware she left the island. He mentioned she had a family matter to tend to?"

He knows more about Elise's absence than I do, but I nod anyway. "I don't know all the details yet. I'm eager to see her. It's been a month."

"I know this past month hasn't been easy on you." The inches between us disappear, and our mouths linger, too close to touching. "But you made it through, my sweet girl. You're stronger than I gave you credit for."

"I've had to be strong." Life started testing the strength of my character at age twelve.

His lips tempt me forward, and I slide my hands along his jaw, fingertips caressing the trimmed beard on his cheeks. Before I can taste him, he backs away, reluctance straining his features. "I'm going to go before I do something foolish, but I'll talk to Landon about carving out some time with you this month." A brief kiss on my cheek is the only goodbye I get.

As the chancellor leaves my quarters, a spark of hope ignites in my chest until I remember Landon's intentions for my future. Because if he intends to marry me off to Sebastian, I can't imagine he'll give Liam permission to see me, let alone touch me.

3

Landon postponed the monthly dinner until the following night, considering Elise's late return to the island. For the past few hours since Liam left, restless energy plagues me. I can't sit still, can't eat, and I can't stop running through various scenarios, each one worse than the last.

Faye said Elise was ill.

The type of sickness that requires treatment off the island? If that's the case, then her return should be a good sign, right?

But what if it's not a good sign? What if she's coming back to say goodbye? What if she's going home afterward because of some horrific life-threatening illness?

I move back to the window seat and tuck my legs under me, determined to settle in for the duration of this nail-biting wait. The last of the sun's rays cast an amber glow over the water, causing the shadows in the room to deepen. I don't bother turning on a lamp.

When Landon enters sometime later, Elise in tow, he

finds me fretting in the dark. Switching on a light, he lets the door shut with an anticlimactic click.

As if this moment isn't one I've been waiting for all day.

I stand, opening my arms to Elise, and she rushes into them. "Are you okay?" I squeeze her for several long moments before pulling back to inspect her. "Faye said you've been ill, but she wouldn't tell me anything else. I've been going crazy with worry."

Elise leads me to the group of couches in the middle of the room. The French doors still stand open, and a chilly breeze drops the temperature inside by several degrees. Landon shuts out the cold before settling onto the couch across from us, Elise taking the cushion by my side.

"I'm sorry for the secrecy," she says, playing with the ends of her short blond hair. "I wanted you to hear it from me." Tears collect in her big blue eyes, and I take her hand in mine, panic building in my chest.

"I'm here," I choke. "Whatever it is, I'm here."

"While you were with Mr. Bordeaux—" Her voice breaks, emotion clogging her throat. "Remember how I was seeing Jerome?"

"I remember." Between my two ladies, Elise was the most excited to come to Zodiac Island. A romantic to the core, she'd had hope in her eyes and innocent dreams in her heart. I used to be that innocent.

Before Liam and his tantalizing touch.

Before Mr. Bordeaux and his cruel conditioning.

Before Sebastian introduced me to the kind of soul-consuming lust I thought only existed in fiction.

"What happened, Elise?"

"Jerome, he...he..." Tears spill over her cheeks, and the rest of her words come out garbled, strangled by pain.

A cold fist of horror grips my heart. "Elise, he *what?*" Though I utter the question, deep down I know the answer. Her face is awash with trauma, her eyes void of the innocence that once lived there.

"He raped me." She exhales a breath, and I wonder if that's the first time she's had the courage to use that word.

I gather her into my arms, and her shoulders shake from the force of her despair. As my lady falls apart, hot drops of distress soaking my sleeve, I turn my attention to the man watching us with grief in his eyes. The rigid set of his jaw spells rage.

"I'm so sorry I wasn't there for you," I say, rubbing her back.

"I said no," she sobs. "It wasn't my fault."

"Of course it wasn't your fault." I veer back and meet her eyes. "Do you hear me? It *wasn't* your fault."

Wiping her cheeks, she nods.

"Has he been punished?" I direct the question at Landon.

A tick goes off in his jaw. "He will be."

"Why hasn't he been arrested yet?"

"Elise didn't tell anyone at first." He hesitates. "Now there's more to consider."

"What is there to consider?" I try to temper my harsh tone but fail. "He sexually assaulted her and needs to be punished."

"There's no question of that." He exchanges a glance with my lady, and she gives a resigned dip of her chin. "Elise has something else to tell you." Landon leans forward, hands clasped between his knees, and I feel like we're back in the library earlier today, in the moments before he dropped the *truth* bomb on me.

"There's more?" I ask, looking to Elise for answers.

Another dip of her chin, then the whispered confession that changes everything. "I'm pregnant."

In the quiet seconds that follow, the weight of her words settle over the three of us with stifling reality.

"Is that why Faye said you were ill?"

Elise nods. "Morning sickness."

"Why did you leave the island?"

"I was going to abort, but…" She looks away in shame. "I couldn't go through with it."

I squeeze her hand. "You decided to keep it?"

"Yes."

"You have my full support."

"Thank you."

"I still don't understand why Jerome isn't in jail."

"No one can know about the assault," Landon speaks up.

I gape at him. "Why not? He can't get away with this!"

"Trust me, my queen. By the time I'm through with him, he'll wish he were in jail."

"So why the secrecy?"

"If Jerome learns of the pregnancy, he could demand to marry her."

"So she'll say *no*, and this time he'll have no choice but to listen."

"You know better than most how the men on this island honor the word *no*." Frustration hardens his tone. "Jerome is a powerful man with strong ties to our government. Now that she's carrying his child, he has a legal right to claim her as his wife."

"Then *do* something about it! Elise can't marry that monster."

A lengthy beat passes as we stare each other down. "I *am* doing something, Novalee. That's why I'm going to marry her myself."

His announcement renders me speechless as I glance between the two of them.

"It's the best way to protect her," he says. "As a member of the Brotherhood, no one will dare contest me when I say the child is mine."

I turn to my lady. "This is what you want?"

Cheeks flushing, she sends Landon a furtive look. "Yes."

"I don't know what to say." I'm grateful to him for looking after Elise, especially since Mr. Bordeaux forbade me from being there for her myself, but my experiences so far have taught me to use extreme caution when trusting the men in this tower.

"We'd like your blessing." The tender look he gives Elise says more than words alone.

"Then you have it."

Landon nods. "Good. We'll also need your support when we announce our engagement to the Brotherhood."

"Of course. Whatever you need."

"Then it's set. Tomorrow night, I'll announce during dinner." Landon rises, his attention on my lady. "But first, the queen and I need to talk to someone."

4

Excited flutters warm my belly as Landon ushers me out of the elevator two floors below the House of Gemini, because I suspect who lives here.

He halts in front of the main entrance—the same style of double doors I've seen on the other floors I've visited. Landon rings the doorbell, and a whole minute passes before Sebastian stands on the threshold, bare-chested and wearing his signature ripped jeans that are so low slung they're almost indecent. The only difference this time is the paint spattering the stonewashed denim.

The displeased curve of his mouth is all too familiar. "What do you want?" Sebastian directs the accusatory question at Landon, though his gaze is on me.

"We need to talk," Landon says, pushing past Sebastian and pulling me behind him. He navigates the lion's lair with ease, as if he's been here a thousand times and the place is as familiar as his own. We come to a stop in a spacious great room that's more art studio than living space. Paintings ranging from abstract to portraits line the walls, shelves hold jars of various-sized brushes and stacked canvases, and a black sheet covers what I assume is his latest work-in-progress. The thing is gigantic, propped upright in front of the wall of windows. It seems Sebastian cares more about his artistic obsession than the incredible ocean view.

I sense him on my heels, the heat of his body radiating from where he's standing behind me, and I tense, caught between needing more space and craving less.

"Since you've invaded my house," he says, voice gruff as his fingers brush the small of my back, "you might as well have a seat."

Shivers shoot up and down my spine as the image of him sitting astride me, fly undone, careens through my mind. I fold into the nearest chair before my knees give out.

Landon smirks. "I can already see this will work out well." There's dry humor in his tone, but underneath that, I detect a hint of amusement.

"I won't even pretend to know what you're talking about." Sebastian drops into the chair next to me. "Do you know what he's talking about, princess?"

My voice is little more than a mutinous whisper. "No."

Of course, it's a lie.

The smile playing on Landon's lips tells me he's not buying my denial. "I'm talking about the sexual tension between the two of you. Careful, Sebastian. You'll knock her up just by looking at her."

"Do you have a reason for interrupting my work?"

Landon pulls a chair across the room and parks it in front of us. Straddling the seat, he rests his arms on the back while his gaze swings back and forth between Sebastian and me.

"I want you to marry Novalee."

Sebastian scoffs. "One day in, and you've already decided you're not interested?" He glances at me with malicious heat in his sea-blue eyes. "Try one of her hand jobs. She's got those down to a science."

"He's a complete and utter ass!" I jump to my feet, mutinous voice no longer an issue, and glare at my *brother*. "And you think this is a good idea? Are you insane?"

"What am I missing?" Sebastian's hooded gaze takes me in from my toes to the blond hair he loves so much. "Other than the ass comment. She's got me there."

"Sit down," Landon orders, his tone taking on a rare edge of harshness. Reluctantly, I obey, biting my tongue as he continues. "How long have we known each other?" he asks Sebastian.

"As long as I can remember."

"That's why I know I can trust you with this." Clearing his throat, Landon surveys the room—as if someone might be hiding behind one of Sebastian's artsy dividers separating the humongous space. "This can't leave the room. *Ever.*"

Sebastian sits up a little straighter, all traces of his obnoxious personality gone. "You know I've got your back." He darts a suspicious glance at me. "But this sounds serious. How do you know you can trust *her*?"

"It involves her. I need to ensure she marries a decent guy."

Sebastian raises a brow. "And that guy isn't you?"

"It can't be me." Landon pauses, three pounding heartbeats sneaking by. "She's my sister."

Sebastian doesn't react at first, and then he *laughs*. "You're fucking with me, right?"

"I'm serious." Landon tells him about the journal, and even about Elise and his promise to marry my lady.

Dead quiet fills the space afterward. Sebastian settles back in his seat, his face marked with stunned contemplation.

"What makes you think I'll win the auction? As much as my father wants it, we all know it won't be easy. My pockets aren't as deep as some in this tower."

"I'm working on it. All I know is I need it to be you. She's my family, and you're the only one I trust to do right by her."

"You know how I feel about this ridiculous tradition." Getting to his feet, Sebastian drags a hand through his hair, his mouth a mean line of irritation. "If the Brotherhood ever finds out about this..."

"They won't."

Sebastian turns on his friend with a scowl. "You sure about that?"

"Yes."

"What if she opens her mouth?" Sebastian jabs a thumb in my direction.

"Too much is at stake, on both sides. She knows this."

Sebastian meets my eyes, and the force of his gaze zooms to my core. But his tone is hostile incarnate. "You really want to marry me, princess?"

"Do I have a choice?" I shoot back. "I have to marry *someone* in this tower."

"What about the chancellor?" He crosses his arms, a perfect example of a half-naked, paint-spattered man failing to hide his jealousy. "You seem to have a thing for him."

"No," Landon interjects.

"It's what he wants." Sebastian nods at me. "Hell, it's what *she* wants."

Landon shakes his head. "It's not going to happen."

"Does the chancellor know that?"

My brother rises and matches Sebastian's height, and the two men stand face-to-face, just inches apart. "In time, he will."

"If I'm going to marry her, don't you think I should have the full story? Because you're not being straight with me."

With a sigh, Landon backs down. "You're right. But the timing is all wrong. Trust me on this."

They both look at me, and my attention ping-pongs back and forth. The probing question I'm dying to ask lingers on my tongue, begging to spring off my lips in search of answers. But I know better.

If Landon won't tell Sebastian whatever secret he still keeps, he's not about to enlighten me.

5

"I still want to serve as your lady," Elise says the next day as she works on my hair, plaiting a basket weave down my back. "For as long as I'm able until the baby is born."

"You'll be a wife soon," I point out, meeting her blue gaze in the vanity mirror. "To a member of the Brotherhood, no less, and from the sounds of it, you'll be busy as his wife."

The three of us shared lunch on the main balcony earlier, taking advantage of the warm temperature. I'd like to think the change of weather is a sign the cold and dreary month under Mr. Bordeaux's rule is behind me, that anxiety won't plague me at the sight of him during dinner.

"I'm clueless of what it means to be the wife of an ambassador." A nervous lilt steals Elise's voice.

She's been high-strung since Landon told us of the role he serves in the Brotherhood. As the Ambassador of Communications, he's a busy man, and no doubt his wife will be expected to plan elaborate dinners and galas for visiting dignitaries. She won't have the time, nor the proper station to serve me in the same capacity we're both used to. As she works her magic on my long locks, reminding me of how I haven't been pampered in a month, the thought of her moving on to the next chapter in her life saddens me.

With Faye gone, I'll miss my friend even more. My reflection hides nothing in the mirror, my expression bleeding distress at the thought of losing Elise.

"I'll make time for you, Novalee. You need a friend you can trust, especially now that Faye has returned home." She steps back, finished with my hair, and I turn on the stool and take her hand.

"I accept your friendship, so long as it doesn't put a strain on your family." I search her face for signs of trauma or guilt, but since she told me about the rape, she's been shut down. "Marrying Landon...is that what you *really* want? Because I'll talk to your parents and make arrangements for you to return home. You don't have to go through with this."

"Can I tell you something?"

"Of course. Come sit with me." I gesture to the ottoman at the end of the king-sized bed, and we settle onto the cushion, side-by-side.

"I've had feelings for Landon from the moment I saw him at that first dinner, but I ignored them because of his title."

I hear all she *doesn't* say.

"And because of your obligation to me." A hint of hurt darts through me. "I wish you'd told me...or Faye."

Maybe if she'd gone to Faye, things would have unfolded differently. It's possible she wouldn't have given Jerome the time of day if she'd believed Landon was an obtainable prospect.

Because Faye might have said something to me earlier about my relation to the Astors. But would my sense of betrayal be any less if I'd heard it from Faye instead of Landon? That's a question I might never have an answer to.

"As your lady, it wasn't my place to tell you."

"I'm more than just your queen, Elise. I consider you family."

Her eyes well, and before the first tear spills, I wrap my arms around her.

"I'm sorry," she mumbles against my shoulder. "I'm going to ruin your dress."

"Don't apologize. It's just a dress. You're more important."

"It's these hormones. I cry over everything now."

"It's more than just hormones," I whisper into her hair. "You've been through so much." What she can't acknowledge is how she has a reason to shed her pain.

It's then I realize we both do.

Iron willpower is my only defense against a breakdown. I blink the tears away and pull myself together. "You'll need to touch up your makeup before dinner," I say, gently wiping the tears from her cheeks.

She nods, rising in a fluid motion, her tears already drying on her skin. Elise is a pillar of strength in that moment, and if I'm half as strong as she is, I'll make it through another dinner with the Brotherhood just fine.

An hour later, I arm myself with that thought as I follow Landon into the dining room on the first floor. With Elise an inspiration at my side and Landon as my shield, I smite down any trace of lingering fear.

Until the sight of Mr. Bordeaux elicits an unexpected knee-jerk reaction. The breath stalls in my lungs as I come to an abrupt stop, my knees trembling with the urge to kneel. Noticing my frozen state just inside the open doors, Landon nods in encouragement.

"You're not in the House of Taurus anymore, my queen. He has no authority over you." He speaks with reassuring confidence as he glances at the man in question, who's already seated at the giant round table of zodiac signs.

Heath Bordeaux doesn't seem to have a care in the world. My presence is inconsequential to him, not even a blip on his radar. If he can forget my existence, I should be able to do the same. I shove the memory of his cold, unbending cruelty to a place deep in my mind and put a lock on it. As my heart rate evens out, I continue to my chair at Landon's side, while Elise slides in next to me.

Another month, another beginning at the altar of this unconventional table. Among the first to arrive, we spend the next several minutes watching the members of the Brotherhood enter.

Liam makes my heart tumble in happiness.

Vance and his reserved demeanor make me nervous, since I'll be his subject next month.

Then Sebastian saunters in and all the activity in the room fades into the background. The sight of him sends a flood of heat to my core. With feigned nonchalance, I cross my legs, pressing my thighs together, and pray my cheeks aren't as hot as my pussy.

This is ridiculous.

I *need* him to touch me...to do more than just touch me. It's the only way I'll get him out of my system.

Sebastian settles in place three seats down, and I swear he's smirking in my direction. I don't have to sneak a peek at him to know it's true.

I feel it.

His smugness wafting in the air. The weight of that aqua gaze casting shivers down my back. The full shape of his mouth. He's so beautiful it hurts.

If I meet Sebastian's eyes, he'll see too much.

If I glance at Liam, he'll see it too.

Instead, I survey the rest of the men gathering around the table. Except for Pax, whose mere existence pulses terror through me, the members of the Brotherhood are strangers—just familiar faces whose names I can't remember.

Virgo.

Libra.

Scorpio.

Sagittarius.

Capricorn.

Aquarius.

Pieces.

That's all I know about the remaining seven men of the Zodiac Brotherhood, save for the monster in the House of Libra.

Servers interrupt my musings by setting the first course in front of me. I've just started on the appetizer, a delectable shrimp cocktail, when Landon rises to his feet.

"I have an announcement to make," he says as his commanding gaze includes every man at the table. "During the last few weeks, the queen's lady and I have spent a lot of time together. I've grown fond of Elise and have asked for her hand in marriage."

A collective series of shocked questions erupts, prompting Liam to stand. He raises a hand and calls for silence.

"Order, please." After the group settles down, the chancellor turns his attention on Landon. "You mean to withdraw from the auction?"

"I do. Elise and I want to marry as soon as possible."

Liam casts a glance my way, and there's no mistaking the curiosity in his expression. "The queen doesn't object?"

"No," Landon answers. "She's given us her blessing."

Liam settles back into his seat, but as he rests his chin on his hand, I recognize his suspicion by the downward curve of his kissable mouth. "Is there a reason you're in such a rush to marry the queen's lady?"

Landon exchanges a glance with Elise. "Aside from being crazy about her?" He pulls his shoulders back and sends a slow glance around the table, taking in each member with an air of bold determination. "She's pregnant with my child."

The reactions are varied, from congratulatory platitudes to ridiculing accusations of impropriety.

Liam raises his hand again, causing the room to go quiet once more. "I see. That is a good reason for haste. Does your father know?"

"I explained the situation. He's given his approval and will inform the legacy members."

"I guess there's only one concern left to discuss," Liam

says. "Do you intend to have physical contact with the queen this month?"

"No. Though I'm certain the queen and I will get to know each other, it will be on a platonic level."

Liam seems relieved, and I wish I could warn him about the bomb Landon's about to drop on him.

"If no one has any objections," Liam begins, "then I don't see an issue with Landon bowing out of the auction."

With the exception of two that appear unpleased by Landon's news, most of the members nod in agreement while a couple wear masks too impenetrable to read, including Sebastian.

Landon clears his throat. "Elise and I plan to visit her home. She would like for me to meet her parents." Pausing a beat, he takes my lady's hand in his. "We'll return in time for the annual Astor Charity Ball."

"I'm assuming the queen will stay here at the estate?" Liam asks.

"Yes. And that brings me to her gift." Landon withdraws a key from his pocket and turns to me. "This opens a room I had renovated just for you. You should have plenty to do while we're gone." He hands me the gold key, and as my fingers grasp the ornate bow, I'm fascinated by the design—a delicate "A" sitting in the middle of the Gemini symbol.

"It's beautiful. What does it open?"

"I'll show you tomorrow. It's a surprise."

"When do you leave the island?" Liam speaks up.

"We leave in two days." Landon takes a sip of his wine, his focus on the chancellor. "I have one final announcement. I've chosen someone as a proxy for the House of Gemini. He has my full, unrestricted permission to spend time with the queen, regardless of my presence in the tower."

Liam's mouth takes on a displeased line. "Who?"

Now it's Sebastian's turn to speak. "That would be me."

"This is absurd," the chancellor says through clenched teeth.

"This is what I want." Landon arches a challenging brow. "No one besides Sebastian has my permission to touch the queen. On this, you will not sway me."

Liam stands, his hands balled at his sides as he passes a glowering gaze between Landon and his rival. Sebastian is the epitome of passion, but Liam Castle doesn't have that thick, coppery hair for nothing.

"You can't just hand her off to someone else for the whole month. That isn't fair to any of us."

"I'm not *handing her off*. She'll remain in the House of Gemini, but Sebastian *will* have free access to her at his discretion."

"Essentially giving him double the time with the queen." Outrage drips from Liam's words.

"Don't pretend you wouldn't jump at the same opportunity, Chancellor." Landon also rises, and the two of them face off across the table. "Or did you already forget about the deal you made with Heath last month?"

I don't understand why, but Landon's reminder makes Liam back down a degree.

"I didn't forget." He flicks an irritated glance at Sebastian. "But he's been unnecessarily rude and obnoxious to Novalee."

Landon laughs. "Most of us are guilty of that. Sebastian

is my choice, and I won't discuss this any further. It's my month, so my word is law."

"I've lost my appetite." Liam storms out of the dining room, leaving a table full of stunned expressions in his wake.

Because the chancellor isn't one to lose his cool, but Sebastian getting his hands on me just sent him over the edge.

6

"You won't give me a hint?" I needle Landon the following afternoon as he leads me down the same hallway as Sebastian's art studio. Whatever his surprise is, I worry it involves his lifelong friend. Instead of stopping at Sebastian's public place of artistry, we continue down the hall.

Landon stops at the last door on the left. "Unlock it."

Withdrawing the key he gave me, I stick it in the lock and turn, and when the door swings open, my jaw drops. It's a large room with an open space concept. Several work stations take up one end while a comfortable seating area and a minibar fill the other. Mannequins and sewing machines line opposite walls, and I realize I'm looking at a fashion design studio.

"Oh, my God," I whisper, crossing the threshold. "You did all of this...for me?"

"I wanted you to have your own space here." Landon waves a hand, encompassing the high windows that allow natural light to spill inside. "There might be some months in which you're forbidden from working in here, but after the auction concludes, you'll have free use of this room."

"It's...wow." I can't find the words to express how grateful and inspired I am by his thoughtful generosity.

"Faye showed me some of your work. It was fantastic. I want you to follow your dreams, so I've hired a team to come in and help. Whatever supplies you need, all you have to do is say the word."

"I'm not sure where to start. Sketching designs has always been a hobby."

"You'll learn. Your team will guide you, and I've got contacts interested in made-to-measure couture. In fact, some of them will be at the ball in three weeks, so your first project should be your dress for the occasion. This is your chance to show off your talent, Novalee."

"I don't know...what to s-say," I stammer, voice choked with emotion.

"You don't have to say anything. You're my family." He sets his hands on my shoulders. "Once your designs gain momentum, we'll talk about opening an exclusive shop on the island. But it all starts here." His gaze bores into me. "Are you ready to work your ass off to make it happen?"

"I'm ready."

"I thought you might be." His lips tilt up in a carefree smile. "I'm hoping you'll be ready for the Fashion Festival in Los Angeles this November. I've already cleared it with Tatum."

"Tatum is from...?" I cycle through the faces stored in my memory, trying to recall the two men whose zodiac signs overlap in November.

"The House of Sagittarius. He's also a pilot. Tatum

agreed to fly you there during his month, if you're prepared by then."

Happiness floods my system, bubbling in my chest before erupting into a smile on my face. Before I give it a second thought, I wrap my arms around him. "Thank you."

He stiffens before slowly returning the hug. "You're welcome."

We break apart moments later, both trying to ignore the resulting awkwardness brought on by my spontaneous hug.

He tilts his head toward the seating area. "How about that conversation I promised you?"

It seems like days since he promised a conversation about my mother's journal, but in actuality, it was during yesterday's lunch that he hinted we still needed to talk. We take seats across from each other, and he settles into his signature pose with his hands clasped between the spread of his knees.

"You read the journal?"

"I did. It wasn't what I was expecting."

"You weren't expecting your father to be in on the affair." It's a statement, not a question, and I answer with a shake of my head.

"Thank you for calling him my father."

"A father is more than DNA, Novalee. It's being present in the middle of the night, wiping away tears after a nightmare. It's wiping your own away because seeing your child in pain hurts you just as much."

"You'll be an excellent father."

"I'm hoping to be an excellent brother too."

I send a cursory glance around the room. "You're excellent in the gift department."

Something passes between us then—a smile, a shared secret, an understanding.

"I'm almost a decade older than you," he says, "and I know how the intricacies of power and greed work. I need you to trust me and follow my lead. I *will* protect you."

My eyes narrow as I try to decipher his expression, because I'm positive he's not referring to his fellow members of the Brotherhood.

There's another threat. I'm certain of it.

"What are you protecting me from?"

"Everything, my queen. The curse of these walls, the iron will of my brothers, but especially the things you don't know about yet."

"Why don't you tell me about them now?" I refrain from crossing my arms, determined to back up my next claim. "I'm a big girl, Landon. Whatever it is, I can handle it."

"You handled the news of your paternity better than I thought you would. I'll give you that." He holds my gaze a beat too long, and the tenuous peace we found splinters as a trace of unease taints the air. "But some secrets are best revealed when the time is right."

"That time isn't now?"

"No, my queen. It's not."

7

Since Landon and Elise left the island, I've been staying busy in the studio, spending the mornings with a private instructor who teaches me about the inner workings of the industry. I never realized there were so many types of fabrics and trims, and before Landon gifted me the opportunity to follow my dream, I had no idea about the mechanics of production or creating a prototype.

Most evenings, I spend my time alone sketching, finding inspiration from magazines and celebrity photos. But my favorite part of the day is after lunch, when my team and I go over my rough sketches, and they give me feedback for improvement, because that's when my designs really start to come together.

On the fifth day, the door to the studio swings open too hard, banging against the wall, and everyone in the room halts, their attention on the figure standing in the doorway.

"Leave us," Sebastian commands, shooting pointed glances at the people surrounding me. Before I can admonish him on his rudeness, the members of my team scurry from the room.

"Was it necessary to speak to them like that?" I stand, hands on my hips, and glare at him.

"No, but it sure was entertaining watching them scatter." With a smirk, he enters and ceremoniously locks the door.

"What do you want, Sebastian?"

Instead of answering, he meanders around the room, fingering the various fabrics. "Landon sure went all out." He whistles as he takes it all in. "Look at this place."

"I'm very thankful for the gift."

"I know you are." He studies me, his head-to-toe scrutiny impossible to ignore. "You're radiant. I've never seen you in your element like this."

That's probably the nicest thing he's ever said to me.

He stops in front of the prototype I've been working on for the last two days. "You made this?" He gestures to the plunging neckline of the halter gown—an azure shade of silk tulle I didn't realize until now matches the brilliance of his eyes.

"I designed it. I've had a lot of help in the production department."

"It's sexy as hell, Novalee." He runs a finger down the chest of the prototype where the appliqué embellished material forms a deep V-neckline that stops above the naval. I'll need strips of fashion tape under my breasts to avoid a wardrobe malfunction. I've never designed anything as provocative as the dress Sebastian's fondling as if it's an extension of me.

I've never worn anything so risqué either, and now I

question my motives, my choice of color, even the way I plan to wear my hair—unhindered by pins or clips and flowing over my bare shoulders.

He's invaded my subconscious like a brain tumor.

He turns to face me with a burning need in his eyes that sucks the breath from my soul.

"Tell me I'll get to see you in this."

Blunt and straight to the point. So like Sebastian.

"I'm wearing it to the ball."

"Ah, yes. The Astor *Birthday Bash of the Year*." His infamous mocking tone permeates the air between us. "Are you wearing it for me, or for the chancellor?" The way he's looking at me, expectation in his gaze, demands an answer.

"For you." I force the confession out as I saunter over to him. "Does that make you happy?" We're only inches apart now, and the heat of his nearness makes me weak. Still, I stand my ground.

"You don't want to know what makes me happy." He grabs me by the shoulders. "But here's a clue—it has nothing to do with a dress."

False bravado is my only defense against him, and I force myself to hold his challenging gaze, even though his hands burn through me like fire. My heart thumps at a furious pace. I'm sure he hears it.

"What *do* you want then?" Strength colors my tone, words falling from my lips with a deceitful, steady cadence. If he notices the tremor in my limbs, he doesn't call me on it.

"What I want has never mattered. We're all victims to the tyranny of tradition and fucking superstition."

"Why don't you leave? Break the cycle for the House of

Leo." Maybe the entire tower would crumble from the missing link that is Sebastian Stone.

"Don't you think I want to?" He pushes forward two steps, turning me toward the wall to the right of us.

"Do you?"

"This place has a way of keeping its prisoners here."

His raw vulnerability digs under my defenses, and before I second-guess myself, I let instinct guide my mouth. At the first touch of my lips on his, he freezes. Three agonizing beats of my heart pass before he lets out a warm breath against my mouth.

"Novalee." My name is a tortured whisper on his breath. He grips me by the hair, but still, he doesn't take the kiss beyond an aching tease.

"Sebastian," I answer, darting my tongue along his lower lip.

Slowly, he backs me into the wall, planting his hands on either side of my face, and I'm reminded of the first time I saw him paint. The way he dominated me in the hallway that day sent me aflutter and now is no different.

He retreats by two inches, and I dart my tongue out again, capturing the focus of his heated gaze.

"Since I'm going to marry you, don't you think it's time I tasted you?"

My lips part, but no words come out. Only shallow breaths rife with longing escape my mouth.

He presses a finger against my lips. "I'm not talking about a kiss."

I'm not sure what he means until he drops to his knees and reaches underneath my skirt to tug at my panties. He pulls them down my thighs, and I can't hold back a gasp. Silky lace surrounds my ankles.

He orders me to step out of the fabric, then he looks up at me with pure desire in his eyes. "Spread your legs."

Oh God. As my thighs part, the bareness of my pussy sends a shiver down my limbs. Gooseflesh rises on my skin, but the space between my legs grows hotter by the second.

"Hold your skirt up and don't let go."

Hands shaking, I grip the light cotton material and raise it above my hips, exposing myself to him.

"Did Liam put his mouth on you?"

"Yes."

"Did he make you come?"

I nod, unable to verbalize my own name at this point.

"How long has it been since you came?"

"Since Liam."

"Jesus Christ, Novalee. No wonder your pussy's begging for my tongue."

His words send a sharp visual spiraling through my mind, and a pleading whimper escapes me. I lose the strength in my knees, and before I melt into a hot, wet puddle on the floor, he grips my thighs, fingers pressing into my skin as he holds me upright.

Our eyes lock. Mine are begging. His are smug.

His tongue runs across his lower lip, and I remember how that lip tasted moments ago, as light and brief as our almost-kiss was.

Just a hint of something sweet.

A tease of something addicting.

Something undeniably Sebastian.

"Do you want me?" It's the most earnest question he's

ever asked me, and maybe I've lost my mind because I'm certain doubt blankets his tone.

"I want you."

No hesitation. No second-guessing or analyzing the hurtful things he's said and done. It might as well be the two of us alone in this tower, because my existence narrows to the man kneeling between my legs as he puts his mouth on me.

"Oh!"

The tip of his tongue circles my opening before gliding to my clit, where he turns me into a trembling mass of bones driven by need. Fisting my skirt, I let my head lull against the wall, lids fluttering closed, and lose myself to the sensory overload of Sebastian's mouth between my legs.

The press of his thumbs dig into my inner thighs, spreading me wide open, and the strength in his upper body is the only reason I'm still on my feet. I'm moaning, my head spinning as perspiration drips between my breasts.

"I...I...need—" The plea fractures with a guttural cry.

"I know what you need," he breathes against my wet slit. "No one will make you come as hard as I will."

The steady licks of his tongue send me reeling. I hold his head between my thighs, my skirt forgotten as it falls where it may, and expel a choppy sonata of breathless cries as I grind on his face in wanton climax.

After the last wave recedes, he veers upright and crushes his mouth on mine. I'm so stunned by the bold move that I gasp and allow his tongue entrance.

It's our first *real* kiss.

And it's laced with the exquisite taste of me on his lips,

accompanied by an aching groan in the back of his throat, infused with a desperate merge neither of us can deny.

He jerks my fingers to the hard ridge behind his fly. "See what you do to me?" His hand covers mine, urging a fast and firm rhythm against his jeans.

"I want to taste you." My demand heats his lips, and they curve into a smile.

"Patience, princess. You'll return the favor." That smile widens with his usual cockiness. "The next time we see each other, you're going to drop to your knees for me. No protests. No hesitation. No *excuses*. I expect you to suck the hell out of me." Mischief illuminates his eyes as he thumbs my kiss-dampened lips. "And I don't care who's around to witness the massive load you're going to swallow."

Speechless.

Unhinged.

Shaking in the aftermath.

That's how he leaves me after giving me the most powerful orgasm of my life.

But on the downward plummet to the cold, harsh ground, a sense of dread takes root because I know he'll make good on his promise.

And he'll do it at the most inopportune time.

8

Sebastian's demand of reciprocity hangs over my head, which makes entering and leaving my studio an anxiety-inducing challenge. A few doors down from where he paints for the public, I scurry in and out of my own space, my breath catching in my lungs every time until I make it behind closed doors.

Because the thought of him catching me in-transit, one of his sexy clients at his side, makes me physically ill. I can't imagine going down on him while a gorgeous model witnesses my humiliation.

I don't want any humiliation at all. I want my first experience of putting my mouth on Sebastian to be as mind blowing for me as I hope it will be for him. I imagine his hands in my hair as I take him between my lips, his faded jeans unzipped and pushed to his thighs, and my knees aching—because of course that's how he'll want me. The mental picture shouldn't get me so worked up, but it does.

Until the vision of Liam intrudes on the fantasy, and I

fret over the possibility of running into *both* of them simultaneously. What a disastrous crash that would be.

And that's why, a few days after Sebastian rocked my world in my studio, I decide to take control of the situation. With Landon and Elise returning tomorrow, I need to do something about Sebastian's insane demand. Though *demand* isn't the right word for it, because he didn't issue an actual order. The command was apparent in his tone.

I set aside my sketchbook, unable to concentrate on my latest design—a summer formal incorporating a feathery pattern down the flowing A-line skirt. The sun set minutes ago, casting the sky in hues of blush rose and burgundy. Nighttime shadows creep into the corners of my sitting room, and I realize how much time I've wasted since the kitchen staff brought me dinner. I've been sitting in my window seat ever since, plagued with a lack of focus thanks to Sebastian.

Nervous flutters dance in my belly as I head into my bedroom and enter the adjacent wardrobe room. I'm not just going to take control of the situation.

I'm going to render him incoherent while I fall at his feet.

This crazy, spontaneous idea might be the only way to break past his defenses while distracting him from his cruel plan of humiliation by way of public indecency.

Desperate times and all of that.

Reaching into the bottom drawer of the tall lingerie chest tucked next to my collection of Louis Vuitton shoes, I pull out a teal lace teddy featuring a thong-cut back. I picked it up on my trip to the island's boutiques during my first month here. The purchase was an impulse buy encouraged by Faye.

Now I'm going to use it as a weapon.

Leaving my hair flowing freely, I touch up my lip gloss and powder my face, then I leave the privacy of my quarters. Only a knee-length jacket conceals the risqué ensemble hugging my body like a second skin. The black stiletto heels on my feet announce my presence in the hall, and I cross my fingers no one else is taking a trip on the elevator.

Luck's in my favor for once, but as I travel two floors down, my knees wobble. They threaten to give out when the elevator doors slide open, revealing the entryway to the House of Leo. I force my feet forward and approach those intimidating double doors.

The zodiac symbol for Leo greets me, the design etched in gold detail as the divide of doors slices it down the middle. The lion fits Sebastian like the lace on my skin; beautiful in simplicity but lethal with sensual power. I imagine him standing in front of an easel, wearing nothing but low-slung jeans and paint spatter, creating his magic with the fire and passion I've come to associate with him.

My fingers inch toward the doorbell, but fear grips my throat, and I falter. This is a bad idea. What was I thinking in coming here, dressed like this? What if he sends me away, his mouth forming that infamous scowl of his? He'll see right through my trick and mock me for my attempt to take control of the situation.

He'll say it doesn't count.

I probably won't get past the threshold.

My feet are already in retreat-mode, literally shaking in my heels, and that's when a stubborn voice shouts through my mind that I'm not the meek, innocent girl I was when I first arrived on the island. The last two months have changed me, the cruelty of the Brotherhood dragging me, kicking and screaming, from the young girl I was into the woman I am now.

A woman that, in this moment, knows exactly what she wants.

I want the lion's surrender, and it won't happen if I keep playing defense. It's time to take the offense and seize the power the men in this tower stole from me.

Bypassing the doorbell, I try the handle and push the door open before I change my mind, because there's no better way to go on the offensive than catching someone off guard.

I want to catch Sebastian Stone so off guard that he falls on his egotistical ass.

My heartbeat drums in my chest as the empty foyer stands before me. Not wanting to announce my presence, I slip off my heels before stepping further into his domain, footsteps careful and quiet as the uncharacteristic act of breaking in roars in my ears.

And maybe that's why I don't hear it until it's too late. The clink of ice cubes against glass, the patter of leather soles on the floor, the scrape of chairs.

And the familiar authoritative tone of the chancellor.

All of it registers just seconds after I set eyes on the group of men conversing in Sebastian's main living space. He's front and center, amusement quirking his lips as he pins me to the spot with his hypnotic stare. That same voice that sent me in here, empowered with blind bravado, now screams at me to flee before his guests turn around and find me on the verge of the room, frozen into a pillar.

Like the foolish woman in the Bible who ignored the warning and suffered the consequences.

Panic takes hold, and I break free, about to turn back the way I came, when Liam cranes his neck and spots me. "What are you doing here?" There's no question of the shock in his expression, followed by the slow descent of angry suspicion that tightens his mouth. The other man also looks over his shoulder, a spectator to the drama unfolding, and I recognize him by his blond ponytail.

Vance. The doctor. The man I'll spend the next month with before the lion ensnares me.

Sebastian grins as he takes me in from my bare feet to the overcoat hiding my lingerie-clad body. "I know why she's here."

"I'm s-sorry," I stutter, feet stumbling back. "I didn't mean to interrupt. I can come back another time." I turn to flee, but Sebastian's words kill any chance I have of getting out of here unscathed.

"I have eyes, princess. I see you, and I sure as hell know you see me. Deal's a deal."

I whirl, sudden anger taking the lead. "There was no *deal*."

He cocks his head. "Wasn't there?"

"There was only you demanding and me not answering."

He shakes his head. "I recall you saying something along the lines of..." He snaps his fingers. "That's right. You said you wanted to taste me."

Liam stands, his fisted hands disappearing into the pockets of his slacks as he looks between Sebastian and me.

"What the hell is going on? What's he talking about, Novalee?"

"That's none of your business," Sebastian answers before I can get a word off my tongue. "You can either stick around for the show, or cut your losses and leave." He gestures toward the foyer behind me. "But if you do, you can forget talks of negotiation."

"Forget it," I tell Sebastian, seething. "I won't play your games."

"You've been playing since we met."

"As of now, the game is over." Turning my back on the three of them, I flee Sebastian's house, gripping my coat as I run for modesty's sake.

I'm in full flight mode, the trip from his floor to mine passing in a frenzied blur. Part of me fears they're coming after me.

Sebastian or Liam. Or both.

Barging into the House of Gemini, I make my way toward my suite. Adrenaline rushes through my veins, and I shed my coat and drape it over a Victorian chair on my way to the ottoman at the end of the bed. My legs refuse to support me any longer, and I crumble.

My erratic breaths charge the air. Sweat lingers on my skin from the mad dash to privacy. My breasts heave in the bodice of the teddy.

I want the scant evidence off my body, shoved in the bottom of the dresser where it should have stayed. This failed attempt at seduction rails through me with equal amounts of shame and frustration, because I'm too much of a trembly mess to make it to my feet long enough to remove the offending garment.

Five minutes haven't passed when I detect the sound of a door opening. I don't hear it shut, but the footsteps that follow tell me someone is inside Landon's home, and it sounds like they're nearing my private quarters.

Another noticeable turn of a door handle confirms my suspicion, and as those footfalls make their way toward my bedroom, where I left the door partially open, I fear I know who it is.

A jean-clad silhouette looms in the doorway, outlined in a halo of light from the lamp in the sitting room. Shadows and heightened emotions settle over my bedroom.

He holds up a pair of stilettos. "You forgot these."

I can't speak as he takes a step into the room where I sleep. I wouldn't know what to say if I tried.

"I had to threaten Liam with a charge of impropriety to keep him from coming in after me." He drops the shoes by the door. "You've got the chancellor wrapped, princess."

Finally, I find my voice. "How did you get in?"

"Walked in, the same way you did when you barged into my meeting."

I'm usually better at locking the main door, especially since I'm here alone. Landon doesn't keep permanent staff on hand, preferring to employ a weekly housekeeper instead. Which means it's just me at night...on a floor sandwiched between too many men with hidden agendas.

"I'm sorry about tonight." With a gulp, I find his eyes in the darkness—a blue luminescence from the moonlight spilling through the windows. "I wanted to be brave."

"Bullshit. You wanted to avoid going down on me around other people." He closes the distance between us, only stopping when he's inches away from brushing my knees. "You don't think I've seen you duck in and out of your studio these past few days?"

My eyes widen. "Why didn't you say something?"

"Because *you* didn't see *me*." He leans down, propping himself on the mattress behind me, and I veer back to avoid contact with his warm, muscular chest.

Because the very essence of him surrounds me, his arms caging me in, the earthy scent of whatever soap he uses filling my nostrils, the intensity of his gaze as it locks with mine. The air between us is heavy with sexual tension, heady with longing, about to bust through the seams of any lingering resistance.

"But you see me now." He sends a leisurely glance down my body. "So this is what you were hiding underneath that coat."

It's not a question. He saw through me the instant his focus landed on me in his house.

"Do you like it?"

"Princess...there's not a man alive who wouldn't." The space between us narrows. "We have unfinished business," he says as his mouth heats my own.

"What are you waiting for?"

Further prompting isn't needed. He pulls his T-shirt off and tosses it on the floor. "Get on your hands and knees."

I look at the space in front of his feet, confusion furrowing my brows, and he tilts my chin up. "On the bench."

As he unbuttons his jeans, I settle into the pose he wants. The short legs on the ottoman puts me at the perfect height to take his cock into my mouth. My hair hangs around my face, a frame for his sexual canvas.

I glance up, darting my tongue across my bottom lip.

"Jesus," he mutters as he pulls down his zipper. "Those lips, Novalee." Wrapping a hand around his erection, he strokes it from base to tip. His thumb swipes the crown and comes away with the evidence of his desire on the pad of that digit, and he pushes it between my lips.

That first taste of him...

The saltiness on his skin.

A flavor that belongs to Sebastian alone.

It's decadent sin.

Withdrawing his thumb, he raises my chin with a gentle touch that brings tears to my eyes.

"You've never hurt me," I whisper.

"That's not true."

"It is. You've been mean, but you've never laid a punishing hand on me."

"Hurting women isn't my thing, but that doesn't mean you should mistake me for a nice guy." Without warning, he pushes his cock between my lips. But the pace he sets is slow, allowing me time to adjust to the hot flesh thrusting against my tongue.

There's a gentleness to the swivel of his hips that borders on lazy, as if he's content to slip in and out of my mouth for the rest of the night, his rhythm a steady buildup that leaves me wanting more. He parts his lips, slides his fingers into my hair, combing it back from my face, and his eyes shutter.

He doesn't speak. Somehow, the absence of words amplifies the charge of sex in the air, heightens the simmering need collecting between my thighs. I can't stand it anymore, and I whimper around his cock, needing...something.

A reaction.

A crack in the wall he's constructed around himself.

Those brilliant blue eyes flutter open again, and I pull back the slightest bit, adding more suction, my tongue swirling around the salty crown of him.

He hisses in a breath.

"You want more of this, don't you?" He follows up the arrogant question with a deeper thrust.

I let out another pleading whimper, and he seats his cock deep, one hand braced on the mattress as he leans over my back. Then he lifts the back of my thong and dips a finger underneath, teasing my anus.

"I want this, Novalee."

His caress turns into a gentle probe that explores rather than conquers, but I stiffen anyway.

"I could take it now," he says, going still in my mouth. "Slip right in where it's so fucking hot and tight." He applies just enough pressure to make me nervous, despite the touch of that finger shooting rivulets of pleasure to my pussy.

I try to pull back, but his hands spear into my hair again. "Relax." Holding me in place, he renews the fervor of his pace, and a satisfied grin shapes his mouth as he plunders mine. "You're not ready for it, but it'll happen soon." The promise hangs between us in the space of five deep thrusts. "I made a deal with Vance tonight for your anal virginity. He's saving it for me."

My eyes widen, and he laughs. "The chancellor wasn't happy about that."

I can imagine Liam's temper flaring, his lack of control

thrown into his face now that he no longer has access to me.

Because Sebastian will never grant it to him.

As he loses himself to the glove of my mouth, his climax only a few noisy thrusts away, I can't help but wonder if Sebastian wants me because he can't resist...or am I just a pawn in the rivalry between him and the chancellor?

With a final jerk, he groans, loud and unrestrained as he shoots his seed down my throat. Afterward, still dripping his completion, he yanks me up by the hair until our lips mash together, and the slow lick of his tongue against mine shakes me apart.

I rake my fingers through his hair, my heart pounding from his kiss as my knees weaken on the ottoman.

"The taste of me on your lips..." He groans into my mouth, then breaks away long enough to tug on my lower lip with his teeth. "You have no idea, princess. No fucking clue."

There's power in his frustration...if only I knew how to wield it.

"Enlighten me." I dart my tongue along the seam of his mouth.

He sucks in a breath. "You're a goddamn temptress." Stepping back, he takes me by the shoulders, ensuring an arm-length distance. "We're done here."

Hurt ricochets through me. "You're leaving?"

"I got what I came for." He leaves me kneeling on the bench in my slinky lingerie while he zips up his pants.

Tears threaten, and I blink to hold them back, determined not to cry over him. He's not worth it. For all of

Liam's flaws—his controlling possessive jealousy—he'd never discard me like this.

With casually cruel detachment.

"Who broke you?" I ask, despising the tremor in my voice.

He freezes, shirt in hand. "The same fucked up institution that'll break you."

"I will *never* break." I get to my feet. "Not for you. Not for anyone."

"You say that now." He pulls the T-shirt over his tousled dark blond hair. "But after a few years, the insidious nature of this place will wear you down."

"What are you talking about?"

"No one's told you yet, have they?"

My heart's pounding too hard, like fists to a punching bag. "Tell me what?"

"You think you're free after the year's up? Think again, princess. This is only the beginning."

9

I greet Landon with a curt, "We need to talk," before he fully enters the House of Gemini. Elise falters at my tone, just two steps in front of her husband-to-be.

"Is everything okay?" she asks.

"It will be as soon as Landon clarifies something."

A sheen of alarm lights her blue eyes. "I'll head down to my quarters and begin packing." Her attention swings back and forth between Landon and me. "He asked me to move into one of the spare bedrooms until the wedding."

"You don't have to pack," he tells her. "We have servants to do it for you."

"I don't mind, and it'll give the two of you time to talk."

With a resigned nod, Landon brushes his lips across her cheek. "I'll come find you soon."

After Elise leaves us alone, Landon gestures for me to follow him into the main sitting area, where he lowers into a chair. "What's going on?"

Too worked up to sit, I pace to the curved wall of windows, a scowl on my face as raindrops squiggle down the glass. The weather is as bipolar here as the personalities of the men in this tower.

"Sebastian told me it doesn't end for me after the auction." I turn around and face my brother, arms crossed. "Is that true?"

Taking a deep breath, he runs a hand down his weary face. "It's true. What did he tell you?"

"He told me next to nothing! Just that this is only the beginning...whatever that means."

Then he left because that's what Sebastian does best after we share an intimate moment. I'm still fuming over his behavior, and it's possible my rocky emotional state is bleeding into this conversation with Landon, but I can't find the will to rein in my anger.

Not after the sleepless night I spent in bed, alternating between the memory of Sebastian's sculpted body standing over me and his parting shot as he left my room.

My feet carry me to the bar set up on one side of the main living area, and though I'm not in the habit of drinking, I pour one now and take a long sip. The amber liquid burns a path down my throat—same as the scorching memory of my encounter with Sebastian.

"You shouldn't be drinking."

I whirl on my brother, alcohol splashing over the rim of the glass. "Don't lecture me on what I should and shouldn't be doing. I want the truth. *All* of it, Landon." It's been two weeks since I learned about my father via my mother's journal—now locked away in Landon's safe, where no one else will read her words and discover the truth.

But there's more to be told. I've sensed it, and Sebastian confirmed it last night.

Displaying the type of patience required of parents, Landon gets up and carefully works the drink from my stubborn grip. "You'll need a clear head when I tell you this."

As he sets the glass on the bar, I let out a slow breath. All the fight seeps from my bones.

"Tell me what?" Now I'm terrified of learning the answer. "It's bad, isn't it?"

His expression tightens with reluctance. "Maybe you should sit down."

I shake my head. "Just tell me."

"After Sebastian wins your hand in the auction—assuming everything goes as planned—he'll have to share you."

"What do you mean *share me*?" My voice goes up an octave. "Isn't that what this year is for?"

Landon casts a glance at his feet. "Sebastian's right. It doesn't end with the auction. Each member of the Brotherhood will have you in his bed for one night during his zodiac month. It's an…ongoing tradition."

My head spins, tumbling end over end with the mental pictures his confession just projected in my mind. "You mean it's a monthly tradition…*every month*, Landon?" Panicked disbelief strangles my throat. "For the rest of my life?"

The downcast nod of his head betrays his shame.

I pivot, fingers gripping the bar, and dry-heave into the sink. He places a hand on my back and rubs in comforting circles.

"I'm sorry, Novalee," he says after I spew what little

food I had in my stomach, since eating was impossible as I waited for him to return and give me answers.

"*Sorry* doesn't help." I turn, shredding him with the accusation in my eyes. "Why can't this...this *sick-and-wrong* tradition be changed?"

"Some members of the Brotherhood have tried to affect change over the years, but the tradition is centuries old." He pauses and takes a deep breath. "And...some of us believe the island is cursed."

Laughter erupts from me—the bitter, disbelieving kind. "You can't be serious."

"What do you know about the history of Zodiac Island?"

"Only what Liam told me. He said Evangeline Castle and twelve explorers founded the island, got rich, then they kept her in a tower and..." My mouth gapes as realization dawns.

"They shared her, Novalee."

"Will I be locked away too?"

"No. The Brotherhood has managed to change some things over the years, hence the queen's monthly duty to the members instead of a free-for-all. The entrapment lies in that duty," he finishes quietly, ashamedly.

"You don't agree with any of this, do you?"

"No, I don't."

"What about Sebastian?"

"He has more reason than anyone to despise the curse we all bear."

"What do you mean?"

"That's his story to tell, Novalee. You'll have to ask him yourself."

I mentally scoff, already knowing the likely outcome of that conversation. "Who issued this supposed curse?" I ask, filing away the subject of Sebastian...for now.

"Evangeline Castle. Some believe she was a witch, and this is her revenge for her wrongful imprisonment by the men in whom she placed her trust. She gave them the world, so to speak, and they repaid her by stealing her freedom."

"But I have nothing to do with that. Why would she make women go through this, generation after generation?"

"Aside from the fact that you *are* a descendent of Evangeline Castle, the historical records we have from that time indicate she went mad. You've heard the saying *misery loves company*? She seethed with so much hatred she would have cursed the whole world if she were capable."

"This is...a lot to take in." My limbs shake with weakness, and I make my way to the nearest chair and collapse into it.

Landon crouches in front of me, an apology clear in the tense lines of his expression. "I'm sorry I didn't tell you sooner. I wasn't sure if Liam told you, and the truth is I chickened out."

I stare at the ocean through the glass, wishing it would sweep me away. "How could you bring me here?"

"It wasn't my decision. My father...*our* father did what he thought was best for you."

"Do you really believe that?" I meet his gaze, brows arched in challenge.

"I don't have an answer, Novalee. Do I want you to endure this burden? Absolutely not."

"Then why did you threaten me when I wanted to leave?"

"Because it's safer for you here."

"Safer? Explain how."

"Your uncle isn't a good man. I'm sure you already know this."

"Did anyone stop to think I'd rather deal with one bad man than a dozen of them?"

"Not everyone in this tower is out to hurt you. You have allies here. You just don't know them yet."

"Is Sebastian an ally?"

"Reluctantly so."

"Because he doesn't like me." The knowledge aches in my throat. "Why doesn't he like me?"

"He wouldn't act so hot-headed and infuriating if he didn't care about you. When Sebastian stops caring, you'll know it because you'll cease to exist to him."

"Then why does he treat me the way he does? His actions aren't that of someone who *cares*."

Lust might drive Sebastian Stone when it comes to me, but I have no doubt in my mind it doesn't go beyond that. The realization sends a scorching needle through the spot in my heart where the lion settled in when I wasn't paying attention.

Things with Liam were simpler.

Safer.

Muted in comparison to what I feel when I'm around Sebastian.

Because he sets me on fire with the touch of his fingers. Sets off my temper with his verbal sparring. And when his vulnerability peeks through during those rare times when I feel like I'm seeing him for the first time...

Really seeing him—the emotionally scarred boy battling demons of which I know nothing about...

That's when he has the most power over me.

Landon takes my hand, and everything about his posture hints at his earnestness. "He cares, Novalee. Just give him some time."

How ironic. Time is all I have. Nine months, to be exact. But will Sebastian be waiting at the end of the auction for me, or will someone else play to win?

Either way, it feels like a massive loss to me.

10

"I can't believe you made this in so little time." Elise gestures at the gown hanging on the rack by the tall windows. A few more alterations and another fitting, and I'll be ready for the ball.

My dress will be, anyway. Me, on the other hand, I'm not so sure about.

"It wasn't all me, Elise. I had six people on my production team who worked tirelessly to bring my design to life."

My lady takes a stroll around the room, eyes wide at what my brother set up for me. This is the first time she's been in my studio.

"It's still a huge accomplishment." She turns to me with a smile—the first one I've seen on her face in days. "You deserve it. I'm glad Landon thought so too."

I've been so busy in the studio since Landon told me the truth about the *queen's duty* that I haven't seen him much.

Though Elise admitted to me last night that he let her in on the secret about my paternity. For such a dangerous secret, he's been busy spreading the word.

First Sebastian, and now my lady.

The latter I trust implicitly. On the former, I hope Landon knows Sebastian as well as he thinks he does.

Because certain men in this tower have shaken my faith in their trustworthiness.

Liam, especially.

After the shock of Landon's revelation wore off, another cold, hard truth hit me. Liam knew all along about the Brotherhood's monthly tradition, and he didn't tell me. I wouldn't expect someone as heartless and stoic as Mr. Bordeaux to care enough to warn me of such a fate, but Liam...

I thought we didn't have secrets between us.

As Elise continues her perusal of my workspace, I tidy up after another long day. My team left two hours ago, but I stayed behind to finalize the details on two of my summer daywear designs. I'm putting away my scattered charcoal pencils when I look up and freeze. A pencil slips from my grip, hitting the table with a louder ruckus than I thought possible for something so small.

Elise turns toward the door where the chancellor stands on the threshold...as if my thoughts from a few moments ago conjured his presence.

"Will you give us a few minutes?" he asks my lady.

She nods before sliding past him into the hall, and I pick up the dropped pencil with feigned nonchalance.

Because anger triggers my heart into an adrenaline-induced rhythm.

"I wanted to talk to you about the other night," he says, shutting the door behind him. But he doesn't lock it like

Sebastian did last week...right before he licked me to insanity.

"What is there to talk about? Sebastian had me against that wall over there," I say, pointing to the spot where his rival had me spread, "and he ate my pussy, giving me the most explosive orgasm I've ever had." I meet the shock in Liam's dark eyes. "I only showed up at his house the other night to return the favor."

Liam says nothing at first, and I can tell he's struggling to formulate a reply. To make sense of my blunt, harsh tone.

"You're upset," he finally says, stepping closer. "Why?"

"Because you *didn't* tell me."

He searches my face, and I pinpoint the exact moment guilt trickles into his expression. He averts his eyes. "You're talking about the queen's monthly duty."

"Is that a question, Chancellor? Or is there something else you haven't told me?"

Bracing his weight with both hands on the table between us, he lets out a sigh of resignation. "I knew this day would come. I just wanted to protect you from it for as long as I could."

"But you can't protect me from this, can you?"

"No."

"Do you believe the island is cursed?"

He looks up with mild surprise. "Yes."

"And this tradition...is it something you accept?"

"It's part of our culture, Novalee. Queens have held this duty for centuries."

"That's not what I asked."

He blinks, and his mouth thins into a frustrated slant. "I

accept it because I have to." He makes his way around the table, and instead of retreating, I stand my ground as his fingers brush my cheek. "Do you think I want you with anyone else?" His tormented gaze shutters for a few moments.

As if he can't stand to look at me knowing I've been intimate with *him*.

Some of my anger seeps from my bones. "I don't know what to think. I care about you both, but *he*—" My voice cracks, and I try again. "He's the one who had the balls to tell me the truth."

"I'm sorry I let you down, my sweet girl."

He truly is, the pain of his betrayal making him bow his head in shame, and I'm reminded once again of how opposite Liam and Sebastian are, despite both of them harboring fire.

Liam and his controlled temper.

Sebastian and his unrestrained passion.

And I'm caught in the middle, a combustible cloud of air between them.

He drops his hand from my cheek, the set of his shoulders dejected. "If I win the auction, I'll have no choice but to share you, but you can always count on my loyalty. *Always*, Novalee."

"What does loyalty mean to you? Does it mean telling me the truth even when you'd rather protect me from it?"

"It means that for as long as you love me back, I'll never touch another. No one else will have my heart, Novalee." A warning sparks in his eyes. "I'm not sure Sebastian can tell you the same."

"Why do you say that?" I retreat a few steps, as if the

backward shuffle of my feet have the power to pull back the question.

He's talking about the models. That has to be it. But just because beautiful women surround Sebastian daily, it doesn't mean he's involved with them.

Last month when he painted my portrait for Mr. Bordeaux, he told me he never wanted the models like he wanted me.

"He'll hurt you, my sweet girl." Liam frowns. "You think you know him, but you don't."

"What don't I know about him, Chancellor?" I cross my arms and wait for an answer, but Liam remains stubbornly silent.

Because the secrets surrounding me inside these curved walls aren't finished with me yet.

11

The doors to the ballroom stand open across from the dining room. Guests decked out in formal wear come and go as soft music drifts into the hallway.

After the dinner portion of the evening, I slipped away and found myself several feet down the hall in front of the portrait of Evangeline Castle. Now I'm riveted to the spot, lingering in the shadows as I stare at the root of this madness.

As if the likeness of her uneasy eyes will explain why she cursed generations of women.

What an absurd thought.

A curse!

I mentally scoff, writing the idea off as an excuse used by men for their unjustifiable behavior. An excuse that spans centuries.

And yet the allure of Evangeline's eyes draw me back in, and I take a step closer. There's something magnetic about her, and it sends a chill down my back. *Is* there a curse hidden in the tilt of her lips? A spell cast long ago to wreak havoc on all future queens of Zodiac Island?

Was this her way of punishing the descendants of the men who wronged her? By making generation after generation fall in love with a queen, only to have to share her every month?

If the legend of Evangeline's curse is true, it's pure genius in cruelty. Insanity in design. Maybe she really did go mad, locked away in that tower with no way to escape.

And maybe I've been in this circular hell for too long that I'm going mad as well.

The clicking of heels against marble draws my attention, and I glance in the opposite direction of the ballroom. A woman materializes from the shadows, her raven hair as sleek as the silk red-wine gown hugging her voluptuous curves.

"Quite the eye-catcher, isn't she?" the woman says, nodding at the portrait of Evangeline Castle.

Surprised by her casual, familiar tone, I blink. "Yes, she's stunning." I study the woman at my side, shuffling through the many faces I saw during dinner, but hers isn't among them. "I don't believe I saw you in there. Are you only now arriving?"

"I like to make an entrance."

Her attire will certainly do the job.

"Your dress is gorgeous. Who designed it?"

"You wouldn't know him. He designs for me exclusively." The upward tilt of her chin prods at my irritation. There's a haughty air about her I don't like.

"And you are?" she asks, smoothing her long hair over one shoulder.

"Novalee Van Buren."

"The queen?" Incredulity laces her question. She sends an assessing glance down my body, the purse of her red lips doing nothing to hide her snub.

"Yes, I'm *the queen*." If she notices my frosty tone, she doesn't show it. I hold her bold, green gaze. "I don't believe we've met."

The music stops, and someone speaks into a microphone about the charity auction, which begins in an hour. The mystery woman in red stares past me to the movement of bodies entering the ballroom.

"Because we haven't." She raises a perfectly arched brow. "If you'll excuse me, I'm late to the party." She struts off in her stilettos, long hair swaying from the motion of her hips, and I can't help but gape at her rudeness.

Taking a few minutes to calm down, I return to the ballroom just as the music resumes. A few guests linger over after-dinner drinks at the round tables set up on the left side of the room. The right side is open for dancing, and I spy Landon and Elise in a tight embrace on the floor, surrounded by other couples. Three sets of French doors stand open so guests can venture into the gardens, enjoying the late spring air.

But there's no sign of the raven-haired woman, and I'm beginning to think I imagined her when Liam sweeps in and takes my hand.

"Dance with me?"

The rules have changed for the night of the ball. He can't kiss me, but he can pull me close and put his hands on me in the name of dancing. So can the eleven other men in this tower, and some of them do. A man with sandy blond hair steals me from Liam's arms.

"Are you enjoying the ball?" he asks, settling his palm on my back. I recall him sitting to Sebastian's left at the monthly dinners.

"I am, thank you." An awkward sense of shyness takes over me. "I'm sorry, I don't remember your name."

"No need to apologize, my queen. It's Miles."

From the House of Virgo.

As he ushers me across the floor with ease, his movements graceful fluidity, I wonder if he's as pure as his sign implies. The haunting strains of the violin falter, and the tempo changes.

Miles passes me off to Vance.

"Only a week to go," he murmurs, pulling me tight against his chest.

I scan the ballroom, on the lookout for Sebastian, since I haven't spotted him since I returned after dinner, but he's nowhere to be found. Neither is the mystery woman, and for reasons I can't pinpoint, that bothers me.

"Sebastian said the two of you made a deal," I say, forcing my gaze on the man in front of me.

He dips his chin. "We did."

"Do you mind if I ask what he gave you in return for my...?" I can't utter the words.

A slow smile plays on his lips. "Your anal virginity?"

Cheeks flushing, I focus on his impeccable bowtie. "Yes."

"You can ask, my queen." He lowers his head, breath warm on my ear. "But I won't answer. I'd rather keep you in suspense."

Liam appears behind Vance and grabs the doctor's attention with a tap on the shoulder. "Mind if I cut in?"

"She's all yours, Chancellor." The man from the House of Cancer steps back with a secret smile, and that's when I spot him.

Sebastian.

And he's *not* alone.

"Who is that?" I ask as Liam pulls me into a sway. My gaze remains on the dark-haired beauty in the red dress, who's leading Sebastian onto the dance floor.

"Who?"

"The woman with Sebastian."

Liam follows my narrow-eyed stare. "That's Lilith Astor."

I falter, mid-step. "Astor...as in the House of Gemini?"

Liam urges my feet into a graceful pace again. "She's Landon's sister."

"He has a sister?"

Liam laughs. "So like him not to mention Lilith." He casts another look across the dance floor, where Sebastian and Lilith move in tandem to the romantic notes coming through the speakers. "Landon and Lilith are twins, but they don't always get along."

Twins...which would explain her sudden presence. The charity ball is in honor of Landon's birthday, after all.

"I didn't realize the House of Gemini took their baby-making duties so literally."

"Twins run in the Astor family. About every other generation produces a set." Liam pulls me closer, and I rest my head on his shoulder. "Have I told you how sexy you look in that dress?"

No, but his sharp stare from across the table at dinner said it for him. "It's not too revealing?"

"*Way* too revealing, Novalee. But I can't find the will to complain." He runs his nose along the slope of my neck. "If I had permission to touch you, I wouldn't be across the room dancing with Lilith Astor right now."

We fall silent, but my mind won't stop spinning with questions.

Why didn't Landon tell me he had a twin sister?

Why didn't she tell me who she was in the hallway?

And why is she clinging to Sebastian like she belongs in his arms?

Something foreign simmers in my blood, casting my vision in the same hue as the woman's mermaid dress. She's gorgeous, older and experienced, and carries herself better than I ever could in a pair of stilettos. Despite the risqué nature of the dress I designed, everything about me screams innocence while she's a walking advertisement for what men want.

I'm inexperienced and childlike…and I'm utterly *jealous*.

"Stop watching," Liam whispers. "It'll hurt less."

Turning my head, I blink. "I don't know what you're talking about."

He tilts my chin up. "You forget I've had plenty of experience watching you lust after him, my sweet girl. I know what's going through your head right now."

"I'm sorry."

"Don't be. It's not your fault."

"I thought I was better at hiding my feelings."

He cradles my cheeks between his warm hands. "Your beautiful face spills all your secrets."

Not all of them. He doesn't know about my relation to the Astors. I bite my lip as it dawns on me.

Because if Landon is my brother, then that means the woman across the room—with her silk-clad body plastered to Sebastian's—is my half-sister.

And I already hate her.

12

Halfway through the auction, Sebastian disappears into the hall with Lilith. Unable to focus on anything but where they might have gone, I fake a headache and tell Landon I'm heading back to my quarters for the night.

As the elevator approaches Sebastian's floor, I'm tempted to stop the car and exit there, but doing so would cause unbearable torture. Because I know they're together, and I can't stand the thought of what they might be doing behind the emblem of that fancy lion guarding the entryway.

So imagine my shock when the elevator doors slide open on the ninth floor, and Lilith steps inside alone. Her sleek locks aren't so sleek anymore, and though she hides it well, her eyes hint at the threat of tears. Casting a glance my way, she reaches for the eleventh floor button, and her fingers halt as she realizes it's already lit.

"Looks like we're headed to the same place," she says, standing back with a lift of her chin.

"It appears so."

"I guess things didn't go well with my brother?" She gives me the side-eye. "Since he'd rather marry your lady."

She has no idea we share the same blood. I wonder if her attitude toward me would change if she knew. Considering which floor she just left, I assume the truth wouldn't make a difference—not with whatever history she shares with Sebastian standing in the way.

It kills me that I know nothing about it.

"Elise's happiness is all that matters," I say, keeping my voice level as endless speculations plague my mind. A muted ding announces our arrival on the eleventh floor. I gesture for her to exit first before following her through the entrance and into the main sitting room.

She makes a beeline for the bar and pours a double shot. "Would the queen of the tower like one?"

"No, thank you."

"Suit yourself." She throws back the clear alcohol—vodka, I'm guessing—and winces from the burn. "Enjoy my suite of rooms while you can."

"Excuse me?"

"Your quarters. They're nice, aren't they?" Bitterness sets her mouth askew. "They used to be mine."

"I wondered why Landon had the space renovated." It's a catty comeback, but I can't seem to rein in my testiness around this woman.

Letting out a dark laugh, she sets the empty shot glass on the bar with an obvious thunk. "Well, I'm going to retire to my guest room. It was lovely to meet you."

"You as well."

If insincerity were an ice-breaker, we'd be the best of friends by now.

She disappears from sight, the quiet click of a door echoing through the semi-dark space, and I glance at the double doors leading to the elevator.

Two floors.

That's all that separates me from the man who can give me answers. The one man I designed this dress for, and he couldn't be bothered to notice me wearing it at the ball. During dinner, he only glanced my way once, and after Lilith showed up...to say the evening didn't go as I'd hoped is an understatement.

I want my dance.

Determination drives my ivory Valentino pumps into action, and I arrive on Sebastian's floor with a fear of rejection coiling my throat. This time, I ring the doorbell, paying heed to the hard lesson I learned about breaking into houses late at night.

He answers wearing dress pants, mussed hair, and a scowl to put the history of scowling to shame. Faint pink lines mark his bare chest like cat scratches.

Or the manicured hands of a woman.

"I didn't get my dance."

With a tilt of his head, he grabs my hand and pulls me inside. We reach his great room, and he brings me flush with his warm chest. The silk tulle of my dress caresses my legs like butter—an exquisite texture against my skin that's only heightened by his nearness.

It's too good to be true.

This unresisting closeness. The absence of our usual

push and pull. The lack of snide banter that serves as an aphrodisiac. Disquiet rolls off him in waves as he holds me.

Because this isn't dancing. This is an embrace between two lovers. A raw emotional connection between two people who need each other.

"Who is she to you?" My voice is breathless enough to count as a whisper.

His harsh sigh is the only clue he heard me. "Someone I thought I was done with."

It's agonizing honesty, and for once I wish he'd lied.

"Do you love her?"

He pulls back, his bright blue gaze dominating mine. "Does it matter?"

I swallow hard. "Why wouldn't it matter?" But I know. Deep down, the reason blazes through my soul, leaving behind a graveyard of ash. His words confirm it.

"Because we can't be together."

This is it. The reason for his hatred. The demon driving his contempt for the Brotherhood and its institution.

Not because it's a sick and wrong practice.

Not because he's an advocate for right versus wrong.

No, it's because he's in love with someone tradition says he can't have.

Instead, he's supposed to marry me...and he hates me for it.

Blind pain floods my vision as I stumble from the warmth of his arms. Why does this hurt so much? Sebastian Stone is callous and cold and cruel...and he doesn't deserve me.

But I want him to.

"What am I to you?"

"Innocent, Novalee. That's what you are."

"That's not what I mean."

"What do you want me to say?" He spreads his arms wide. "You have no choice but to marry me. Nothing else matters."

I shake my head, sending two salty drops trailing down my cheeks. "It's the other way around. You're forced to marry *me*."

"Like I said..." He closes the distance and palms my cheek, his thumb wiping away a tear. "The mechanics don't mean shit. It doesn't change anything."

Gripping his wrist, I push him away. "I don't want to marry someone who hates me."

"I don't hate you."

"But you love *her*."

"And you have a thing for the chancellor. Do you not realize what knowing that does to me?"

"I didn't know you cared."

"Jesus. You should have. The shit going through your mind right now about Lilith? Turn it around, princess. Then maybe you'll see what I'm talking about. You're not the only one screwed up in the head over this."

"You and me..." I look at him through my tears. "We're a destructive combination."

"There isn't much we can do about it."

"Yes, there is." I straighten my spine. "Landon needs to pick someone else to win."

Sebastian scowls. "You want the chancellor."

"This isn't about Liam."

"The hell it's not."

"It's about *you*."

"Me?" he says, his voice a deep, accusing gruff. "Am I not good enough for you, princess?"

"I want someone who wants me back."

"You think I don't?"

"I think your heart and dick are two separate entities that can't agree on anything."

He lowers his attention to my chest and the expanse of skin there, and his aqua eyes deepen. "My dick wants to use that dress for what it was designed for."

He's dangling subject-changing bait, and I can't help but take it. "As the designer, I'll need an example."

"Two slides of that material, and I'd have your tits in my hands. Have you ever had a man's cock between them?"

I gasp, indignant. "I put my heart and soul into this dress, and that's all you have to say about it?"

"I'm a man with eyes, princess, and a cock that aches for you to the point of distraction." His voice rises, sending me into retreat mode, but he follows with a predatory gait. "I want to invade *every* part of you."

He wants my virginity—on both counts. But that's all he wants, and the reminder renews the searing ache in my chest.

"So I get your cock, but she gets your heart?"

"It's not a total loss," he says with a sneer. "You get Liam's. Everybody fucking wins."

"We're done here." I whirl, intending to make my escape through the door, but his hand stops me, electric fingers gripping my arm.

"We'll never be done, princess."

I glare at him over my shoulder and toss his words from over a week ago into his face. "I got what I came for."

Confirmation.

Heartache.

And the need to have a talk with my brother about my future.

13

Lilith Astor swept into the tower long enough to destroy and conquer, then she disappeared just as suddenly. Three days before I'm scheduled to move into the House of Cancer, I find Landon alone in his home office.

"Where's Elise?" I ask.

"She's exhausted from all the wedding planning." The *tap-tap-tap* of fingers on his keyboard signals his distraction. "She went to lie down for a while."

I step in and shut the door behind me. "I wanted to talk to you alone."

My serious tone grabs his attention. He looks up from the laptop and removes his reading glasses. I never realized until now that he wears a pair. My brother, the studious ambassador.

"What's on your mind?"

"It's about Lilith."

Leaning back, he runs a hand through his dark hair. The length has grown longer in the last month. "Why don't you take a seat?" He gestures to a chair tucked against the wall.

I pull it to the front of his desk and settle in for what I expect will be an uncomfortable conversation. "Why didn't you tell me you have a twin sister?"

"Technically, you and I *both* have a sister."

I give him a pointed look. "A sister I knew nothing about until Liam told me who she was."

Landon winces. "I should have told you, but things are complicated with Lilith. She's...difficult to handle."

I got a firsthand taste of her difficult nature, but I don't tell him that.

"Is she coming back?"

He shrugs. "It's hard to know what Lilith will do."

I gather courage for my next question. "What's the deal with her and Sebastian?"

Slowly he nods, understanding coming to light. "You want to know if they're still involved."

"Yes."

Because as much as I hate it, Lilith Astor is an intolerable wall standing between any real union with Sebastian, and though marriage to a man in this tower isn't something I'd chose for myself, I want it to be real.

I want it to be reciprocated.

"It's an obsolete question, Novalee. He's going to marry *you*."

"Not by choice."

Landon frowns. "Is that what he told you?"

"Not in so many words. But I'm not as gullible as you might believe. He wants Lilith."

"Sebastian doesn't know what he wants." He shakes his head. "And you've got the wrong idea about him and Lilith."

"That may be so, but I think it's only fair you change

this marriage scheme of yours." Not that I pretend to know how he plans to make it happen. "I want Liam to be an option."

"Absolutely not."

"Give me a logical reason why."

"I don't trust him."

"He's always been kind, and he looks out for my best interests."

"Or he's looking out for his own."

I narrow my eyes. "Whatever you're holding back..." I wave a hand around his workspace. "Now's the time, Landon. I'm leaving in three days."

A lengthy beat passes as he studies me. "Perhaps you're right."

My shoulders relax as I watch him stride to the wall opposite the tall mullion windows. He slips his hand underneath a shelf on a bookcase filled with volumes of what appear to be reference books. Three seconds later, a landscape portrait of the ocean slides to the left, revealing a safe. After the security panel scans his fingerprints, the gears shift and the door opens.

My eyes are wide by the time he returns to the desk. With an air of significance, he sets an envelope on the surface between us.

"What's that?" I stare at the letter-sized envelope, trepidation stiffening my muscles.

"It's a letter your father sent mine." He slides it to me. "Dated the week before your parents' plane went down."

I push it away. "Just tell me what's inside."

"Very well." With a sigh, he settles back into his seat. "King Van Buren asked my father to ensure the safety of you and your nation...should something happen to him and his wife."

I blink rapidly as Landon's words filter through my brain in disjointed confusion.

Ensure the safety of you...should something happen...dated the week before...

"You're telling me—?" My voice cracks, unable to put the implication into thought, let alone words.

"We don't believe the plane crash was an accident. Someone conspired to have your parents assassinated."

"Rowan?" I choke out as hot devastation bleeds from my eyes.

"We believe so."

My mind flashes back to when I was under the thumb of a harsh, uncaring uncle who only saw me as a means to an end. A man who might have killed my parents. "Why did your father leave me there with him? For *six years*, Landon."

"He did it to protect you."

"Protect me?" I scoff. "Well, he failed."

"No, he didn't, Novalee. My father used the auction to make you valuable to Rowan, all while preserving the secret of your paternity, and that meant you were safe."

"Safe from what?"

"The same fate as your parents."

I hold my stomach, about to be sick. "He wants the throne."

"Yes. We think he'll attempt to have you assassinated after the auction."

"But whoever I marry will be the king consort. He'd have to get rid of us both."

Landon clenches his jaw. "Not if the man you marry is working with Rowan."

I gape at him as it dawns on me. "All he'd have to do is abdicate, and my uncle would become king." Rising on shaky legs, I pace in front of Landon's desk as my world once again rumbles under my feet. "But what makes you think Rowan's working with someone in the Brotherhood?"

He taps the letter on his desk. "The king discovered the plot. That's why he contacted my father for help."

I place a hand over my galloping heartbeat. "You know who it is, don't you?"

He nods, mouth a grim line as an apology lights his emerald eyes. "Rowan was in contact with Chancellor Castle in the weeks leading up to the crash."

"*Liam's* father?" My voice is high-pitched, disbelieving. Instantly, my heart denies it. "No! That can't be right."

"It's true, my queen."

Landon's certainty quakes underneath me, and that's when the ground fissures. I fold into the chair before my feet slip through the cracks.

Because Liam Castle isn't the safe haven I thought he was.

THE SAGA CONTINUES

www.authorgemmajames.com/books

ABOUT THE AUTHOR

Gemma James is a *USA Today* bestselling author of sexy contemporary and dark romance. She loves to explore the darker side of human nature in her fiction, and she's morbidly curious about anything dark and edgy, from deviant seduction to fascinating villains. Readers have described her stories as being "not for the faint of heart."

She warns you to heed their words! Her playground isn't full of rainbows and kittens, though she loves both. She lives in Oregon with her husband and children, a gaggle of animals, and bipolar weather.

Visit Gemma's website for more info on her books:
www.authorgemmajames.com

Printed in Great Britain
by Amazon